The Lady of Fortune

Anne R Bailey

INKBLOT
P·R·E·S·S

Ebook ISBN: 978-1-990156-25-0

Paperback ISBN: 978-1-990156-26-7

For my writing group. You encouraged me and then gave me a shove when I needed it.

ALSO BY ANNE R BAILEY

Ladies of the Golden Age

Countess of Intrigue

The Pirate Lord's Wife

The Lady of Fortune

Forgotten Women of History

Joan

Fortuna's Queen

Thyra

Royal Court Series

The Lady Carey

The Lady's Crown

The Lady's Ambition

The Lady's Gamble

The Lady's Defiance

Bluehaven Series

The Widowed Bride

Choosing Him

Other

The Stars Above

You can also follow the author at: www.inkblotpressco.ca

PROLOGUE

It is hard to focus on threading my needle when a large beetle keeps colliding against the windowpane, desperate to escape.

Thud. Thud.

It sounds like it might injure itself in the attempt. I can understand its desperation. Who would want to be trapped in this miserable castle longer than necessary?

I envy the creature as it finally finds a crevice and flees. Would I ever leave? I was only seven years old, but I already knew my prospects were dim.

My hand smooths over the homespun wool of my skirt. I should be dressed in fine silks. After all, I am descended from two royal bloodlines—Plantagenet and York. But there is no money for finery anymore. Now we are grateful when we can keep a fire burning in the grate.

Long before I was born, my grandfather, the Duke of Buckingham, died on Tower Hill for threatening the king's power and, if rumours are true, seeking to claim the throne. His actions were nothing short of treason. So my father, instead of inheriting a dukedom and all the Stafford wealth, had to be content to walk away with his life.

I thought this was unfair. My parents had done nothing wrong, but I hadn't been there to complain. Not that anyone would have listened.

Everywhere I look, I see hints of a glorious past, from the faded tapestries to the heraldic symbols carved into stone. I know there are trunks and chests in the cellar containing court dresses and rich linens tucked away as we wait for better times. My parents are still proud of their heritage and dream of returning to court. They cling to the little that remains, but for how much longer can we go on? Every year, we are forced to sell our precious heirlooms to ensure we have food in our bellies. After the last remnants of our glory are gone, what will become of us?

Last spring, when the roof leaked, my mother's diamond necklace was used to pay for the repairs and outstanding debts to the crown. If the crops fail this year or some other tragedy befalls us, will we be able to find something of value to sell? Worry gnaws at me.

"Daydreaming, again?"

I snap out of my thoughts to see my mother peering down at me.

"Working." I hold up the embroidery I have been struggling with. A pattern of red roses shines against the beige cloth.

Her lips purse into a thin line of disapproval. "You were supposed to be practicing stitches."

The tightness in her tone warns me she is upset.

"I know. I just thought I could copy the pattern on your petticoat. The one you wore last Christmas. It was so beautiful and..."

Her finger runs over my work. I know it isn't perfect. Far from it. I haven't quite mastered the loops and tight stitches required to make the roses. Nor do I think I used the right colours for the leaves and shading.

"If you insist on jumping ahead in your lessons, then you shall keep working until you achieve perfection. Pull out every stitch and begin again."

"But mother—" The protest dies on my lips at her pinched expression. Today is not the day to argue with her.

She takes a seat close to the window and picks up her own needlework.

We are a large family and, judging from the swell of my mother's belly, we will grow even larger. I might be the fourth of seven children, but as one of two daughters, I am a rarity. My eldest sister's poor eyesight keeps her confided to the nursery and means I have our mother's undivided attention and tutelage.

At the moment, she is working on one of my father's linen shirts. I envy the intricate black embroidery stitched neatly into the collar. It is my mother's own work, something she learned years ago at the court of Queen Catherine. I am desperate for her to teach me. But even if she wasn't angry with me right now, black thread is expensive and there is no money for such frivolity.

For a time, we work side by side in silence until the sun begins to dip on the horizon. With it comes the noise and bustle of the household preparing for the evening. We hear the clattering of hooves and the shouts of my two older brothers as they ride into the courtyard with my father in tow. By now, they should've been sent to a great noble house to complete their education. But who would be foolish enough to befriend a family tainted by treason? What benefit could there be to allying with a struggling family?

My mother sets down her own needle and looks over at me. I have finished taking out the stitches. My fingers, quick and nimble, undid what had been hours of needlework.

"Go get ready for supper and tell Margaret to come down as well." My mother dismisses me.

I almost protest, but when I blink, I feel the strain in my eyes. Even my back is stiff from sitting for so many hours. There is something pensive in the way she tilts her head to look out the window. As I leave, I catch her sad expression as she rubs her belly and continues to stare out at the darkening sky outside.

Every moment of our lives is laced with regret and bitterness. The knowledge of what could've been is a hard pill to swallow. Even for me.

Two days later, we receive an unexpected visitor.

My aunt, the Duchess of Norfolk, slides from her

horse with a confidence and ease any knight would envy. She stares at us, arranged as we are in the courtyard, with pity. Only when her gaze settles on her brother does she smile.

With less than a year between them, they were inseparable in their early years. A tight bond had grown between them that distance and time could not rip asunder.

He steps forward, bidding her welcome to his home. A few years ago, she would have been giving him precedence. But now she is a duchess, and he is a mere lord with barely a penny to his name.

Her sharp critical gaze softens. "Harry, you don't need to be so formal with me," she says, as she steps forward and kisses both his cheeks before moving on to embrace my mother.

"Are you travelling north?" my mother asks, observing the retinue that accompanies my aunt. "I thought you'd be entrenched in London."

"As it happens, I am returning to Suffolk for a time. We shall speak more inside, where we won't be overheard," she says, her eyes catching mine.

Both my parents spin around and frown at me.

My cheeks redden as my aunt approaches.

"There is nothing wrong with listening in on others' conversations. Provided you don't get caught." At that, she chucks me under my chin.

I return her smile and curtsey to her, my movements graceful and the correct height for a lady of her rank.

"Well done," she says.

My mother hasn't failed to teach me courtly manners. At my side, I can feel Margaret stiffen. She is the quiet one, and I always steal the spotlight that rightfully belongs to her as the older sister. It isn't something I set out to do, and I am sorry if it bruises her pride to be overlooked.

That night, we dine in private, and after the meal is done, my father dismisses the servants. Finally, we are alone.

"Tell me, Margaret, do you play the virginals?" my aunt asks.

Margaret's cheeks go pink with pleasure as she nods.

"Will you play something for me now? I should dearly love to hear you."

"Of course." Margaret curtseys and rushes to get her instrument.

It isn't long before music fills the room. She might only be thirteen, but Margaret is already an accomplished musician. Before our family's disgrace, she delighted Queen Catherine with her playing and took lessons with Princess Mary.

The adults don't listen passively to her playing. They sit, heads pressed together, imparting news they don't wish to be overheard by spies at the keyhole. I am on my mother's left and do my best to keep still, hoping they will go on forgetting I am there.

"That whore has arranged my daughter's marriage," my aunt begins. "My poor Mary is to be wasted on Henry Fitzroy. I told my husband I would never agree to the match, but of course, my opinion counts for nothing." She lets out a heavy sigh. "And the poor queen... they keep moving her from castle to castle, each worse than the last. They aren't satisfied with stripping her of her dignity and titles. They are taking everything. Her jewels, her barge, her ladies-in-waiting. She's a prisoner, unable to see her daughter or the Spanish ambassador. It's disgraceful how she's being treated."

My aunt is speaking of Catherine of Aragon, the Spanish queen, whom the king is intent on divorcing. By all accounts, my aunt should support him. The Howards stand to gain untold wealth and influence at court if the king succeeds in casting her aside and marrying Anne Boleyn, her husband's niece. However, my aunt is loyal and holds strong convictions. Anne Boleyn might be her niece, but she is a mere knight's daughter. Even worse is the fact that the Boleyns are descended from merchants, hardly worthy of marrying royalty.

I imagine it torments my aunt that someone of Anne's low breeding is now set above her.

"So you took yourself away from court to show your displeasure?" my father asks, his eyes full of mirth.

My aunt's curt nod tells him everything. "The official reason is that I am preparing Mary's dowry and gathering some heirlooms from the coffers at Kenninghall."

"Something you could've asked a servant to do for you." My father shakes his head. "You are playing with fire. Wouldn't it be better if you befriended the future queen? Think of what you are risking by insulting her like this."

She gives him a scornful look.

"You shall not lecture me, Henry," she says, imperious. "Between the two of us, I am the one who still holds a title and isn't living in some decrepit castle."

That stings. My father's eyes narrow, but he recovers his good humour quickly. "You are welcome to find more suitable accommodations elsewhere," he dares her.

I wonder at my father's bravery. But then again, they are siblings and have needled and teased each other for decades.

"We do apologise for not being able to entertain you as befits your station," my mother says, happy to play the part of peacemaker.

"Nonsense. My niece's playing is lovely. Her breeding shows in her talent. It was a stroke of bad luck that you and yours are not where you belong. Once Anne loses the king's favour and is cast aside, perhaps he will see sense. He cannot continue promoting every lowborn person who can string together enough words to form a sentence." She bites her lower lip, casting a glance around the room to reassure herself we are alone.

I sit back in my seat, wondering who she is talking about. The conversation continues in hushed whispers, and even I can no longer hear them.

Margaret plays for half an hour before her fingers falter. It has been a long day. My mother nods to her to set aside her instrument and take a seat with us.

"I stopped by with another proposition in mind," my aunt says. "I want to offer to take Margaret and Dorothy. They shall join my household and be given a proper education. I shall arrange good marriages for them and bring them to court as often as is fitting."

My heart skips a beat. I cannot believe what she has just said. My eyes go wide as I glance from my parents to my aunt.

She chuckles. "This one is excited. Tell me Dorothy, do you dream of going to London? Bumping shoulders with the great people of this land?"

I can hear the mocking tone in her voice and lower my eyes.

Again, she chuckles. "I hope it never disappoints you, niece."

"Never," I say with such fervour that she is taken aback.

She glances at my father. "She will wilt if you keep her here tucked away in the country."

"It isn't by choice that we are living here like this." I hear the bitterness in his voice as he says this.

"Then let me help you."

He groans. "I wish you could speak to the king. Your husband, perhaps..."

"I know, Henry," she says, reaching over to pat his hand. "But I'm afraid even if my husband were inclined to help, it would be beyond his powers to get your titles and lands restored to you. I wish there was more I could do."

My mother dismisses us so the adults can speak freely without us children.

I have to pinch my wrist to hold back a protest. How can we be sent away at such a crucial time? I need to know if I am to become my aunt's maid-in-waiting. All my dreams might be within reach. On a whim, my aunt has changed the course of my destiny. I regard her in a new light. She is a powerful force unlike any I have ever encountered. What would it be like to wield that sort of influence? Then another more terrifying thought strikes me. What if she changes her mind?

For a while, it appears she has. The following day, my aunt leaves without a word to me or Margaret. My parents are in a contemplative mood but say nothing. The news from London is bad and they worry war might come to England's shores. I hate the spark of hopefulness that bloomed in my heart last night. Will I never escape my dreary home?

A week later, I see I was wrong to despair. An armed guard arrives to convey Margaret and me to Kenninghall. My sister cries as we bid farewell to our parents and leave Staffordshire behind. I pat her back attempting to console her, but I am thrilled to be leaving and unable to sit still on my cushioned seat.

PART I
25 YEARS LATER

CHAPTER 1

1558

"God bless," I say, passing a neighbour as I hurry through the streets of Basel. My maid struggles to keep up with me.

I am a girl again, heart thumping wildly as I head home. My thick chestnut hair is tucked neatly beneath a starched white cap. I want to pull it off and let my hair fall loosely down my back, just as I want to cast aside the dark dress with slashed sleeves for one of bright yellow.

For the first time in years, hope fills me, giving way to joy.

Can the others I pass on the street not see that everything is about to change? I want to laugh and shout out my good news.

Thankfully, I do none of these things. My exile is coming to an end. The last thing I need now is to be labelled a madwoman.

I continue down the cobbled streets, forcing myself not to smile. There is nothing about my appearance that sets me apart from the throngs of other women in this city. I am neither beautiful nor ugly, and I dress modestly. I am tall, and with even features. Fine lines don't mar my face, though this year I will be thirty-two. It is a vanity that I noticed, and I quickly cast the thought aside.

In my childhood, my aunt valued my wit. Later my husband, valued my stoutness and bravery. Given how we were forced to flee England and make a new home in this distant land, those were more valuable traits than possessing a pretty face.

Poor William. I miss him still. We'd married at my aunt's bidding, but tenderness grew over the years. We were partners in everything. He wasn't proud like other men and often asked for my opinion and advice.

When the heresy laws returned to England, he wondered if we should flee. It was I who encouraged him. We could not hesitate, not when the safety of our children was in question. I reminded him we could always return, and he made a solemn vow that we would. Our plans to flee were made in secret. I didn't even tell my brother, Henry, or my parents. Were they surprised when my letters arrived informing them my family and I had fled? I wish I knew how they fared. But I refused to put them at risk by contacting them.

Year after year passed, and I waited. We were so certain we would return to England soon. Surely, Queen Mary would see the error of her ways. On his deathbed, my husband took my hand and made me promise our children would one day return to the land of their birth.

How could I deny him? After all, it was my greatest wish as well.

After his death, my comely features and royal pedigree—tainted as it was—ensured I received several offers of marriage. I turned them away. With enough wealth to provide for myself and five children, I was not in a rush to accept anyone. Instead, I retired from the bustling city of Geneva to Basel. My situation was unusual and frowned upon. I was too young to be allowed to live the rest of my life as a respected widow. Yet, how could I forget the promise I made to my husband? I knew if I laid down roots here, I would never leave.

Now as I rush home, the letter I hold clutched in my hand will confirm I was right to wait. Queen Mary is dying with only one heir to come after her: the Protestant Princess Elizabeth. Who also happens to be my distant cousin. The tides are finally changing in my favour.

As I enter my modest home, I see John Calvin, my protector and the godfather to my youngest son, has preceded me. He is waiting, warming his hands by the stove, as Edward, my eldest son, recites his Psalms in perfect French.

John Calvin's eyes are closed in silent contemplation and appreciation.

I stop in my tracks and curtsey politely to him. He nods in my direction, but we don't speak until Edward finishes his recitation.

"Very good, Edward," John Calvin says, his eyes sincere. "Keep at your studies and don't let me hear you are running with the likes of Simon at the market again."

I gape at my son. He is only seven. How did he escape his tutor? And how did John Calvin know when I did not?

"I told you, Lady Dorothy, that you need help," he says, turning to face me.

To hide my defiant expression, I bow my head. I am grateful to him, but we disagree when it comes to the subject of my future.

"Good day, sir," I say politely. "What brings you to my home today? May I offer you any refreshment?"

He gives a shake of his head. "Edward, why don't you go read to your brothers while I speak to your mother?"

My son bows his head, but I can tell from the drop of his shoulders that he is sulking. Despite his tendency for mischief, he idolises John Calvin and doesn't want to be sent from his side.

I turn my attention back to the imposing man. The plain black robes he wears are misleading. For years now, he's held office as leader of the Church of Geneva, ruling and defending the great city as any King might. He continues to be a respected theologian and scholar.

My husband did well when he befriended this great man upon our arrival in Geneva. Though it would've been hard not to. John Calvin is an inspiration and William worked for him out of true devotion and belief in his vision of the future. His loyalty didn't go unnoticed, as is evidenced by Calvin's continued willingness to look after us.

"Won't you sit?" he says. This might be my home, but he has precedence here. I know this won't be a quick conversation, and though I'm aching to reread the letter in my hand, I do as he asks.

His serious expression breaks into a soft smile as he regards me before taking a seat at the table across from me.

The table is plain and unadorned, though I have ensured it is polished and smelling of sandalwood. Everything in this house is plain. However, I still have my pride. I ensure the walls are freshly whitewashed every year, and the floors are kept clean. Only a plain wooden cross breaks the monotony of our bare walls and floors. Who would've thought I would miss the faded tapestries of my old home?

In England, it would embarrass me to invite a man of such importance into this house, but I am sure I would find John Calvin's own home just as sparsely decorated and furnished. The Protestants in this land live plainly. Decadence and frivolity are abhorred.

"I know the news you must have received today," he begins. "For I have received a letter as well and have come to discuss a few things with you. Seeing the spark in your eye as you entered, I can already tell your first inclination will be to board the first boat to England."

I wait as he considers his next words. Age has ingrained the power of patience in me. I won't speak out and needlessly enter into conflict without hearing what he has to say.

"I am assured by my contacts that the Queen of England doesn't have long to live. She might be dead and buried in the time it took for us to receive this news."

I nod.

"This means that her sister will inherit. We all know her secret inclinations to Protestantism, but she has also attended the Catholic Mass."

"I have heard they forced her to. She postponed as long as she could. Her own sister accused her of being a heretic and would've killed her."

John Calvin inclines his head, stroking his long beard.

"Still. There is doubt in my mind what she will do now that she will be queen and even further doubt about whether she will be capable of ruling the kingdom. There are rumours the King of Spain will offer to marry her..."

I choke back a scoff. "But that is ridiculous. King Henry—"

He holds up his wrinkled hand. "I know. The marriage would be invalid even if they get a dispensation from the Pope. Do you think Princess Elizabeth will be able to refuse? Would Phillip not threaten to invade England? He had no qualms about bringing the Spanish inquisition into the country."

I've never had the pleasure of meeting Princess Elizabeth. Everything I know comes from gossip. There's a tight knot forming in my stomach as my initial joy is being tempered by reality.

"It is possible that England will become a great Protestant nation, something that would have been achieved had King Edward not died at such a young age. We cannot forget that Queen Mary has Catholics entrenched at every level of government. They may even prevent Princess Elizabeth from being crowned. It's easy to surmise that the future queen will face powerful opposition if she wishes to follow the true faith."

I flinch, clutching my hands in front of me to keep from trembling in disappointment.

"So I wish you to reconsider your plans to return to England. Here, you can have a life safe from persecution. I will teach your sons at my college and they will grow up to have fruitful careers. Your daughters will marry well. I will see to it. You could remarry as well. There are plenty of good men who would be honoured to marry you. I know you still grieve for William but that doesn't mean you should be alone for the rest of your life."

I hang my head low. How can I explain to him I prefer to remain unmarried? After a moment's silence, I say, "if I choose to leave, will you still give me your blessing? Or would you prevent me?"

He clears his throat. I imagine he's giving my question serious consideration.

"You would have my blessing, Lady Dorothy. I promised your husband I would support you, whatever your decision. Unless, of course, I think it will put your immortal soul in peril," he adds.

"You are too kind and generous," I say, looking up into his kind face. "I will consider what you have said.

This is a letter from my aunt," I say, placing it on the table and sliding it towards him. "You may read it if you wish. My children and I shall be welcome if we decide to return. I don't think she would dare even write to me if it wasn't safe to do so."

His brow wrinkles in obvious displeasure. "The Duchess of Norfolk is a staunch Catholic," he reminds me gently, as if I could have forgotten.

"But above all, she's a pragmatist. And who knows what she believes after all these years? Even she wouldn't have condoned the actions of Queen Mary. How many perished unjustly at the stake because of the queen's overzealousness?" I shake my head, grateful again that we left when we did.

"Very well. Then regardless of what you decide, may God be with you."

"And with you."

I force myself to wait a week before making my final decision.

It grows harder to wait as more and more news reaches us from England and other English refugees began preparing to return to those distant shores. I know that I cannot remain here. Geneva will never truly be my home.

As promised, John Calvin doesn't stand in my way.

"You wouldn't consider leaving John in my care,

would you?" he asks, despite already knowing my answer.

"You are welcome to join us, sir," I smile in response. "But he is too young to be separated from me. Perhaps, when he is old enough to attend university, I will send him to study under your fine tutelage. If you will accept him."

"You seek to flatter me, Lady Dorothy," he says. "Well, rest assured that I think he will make a fine scholar, and I eagerly await the day of his return."

"Will you stay for supper?" I say, but he is already on his feet. He is an important man and cannot dally for long.

Since I have decided to return to England, he has graciously stepped in to help me arrange safe passage for my family. It will be a long journey by land and sea, one I am dreading to take as the day approaches.

But first there is the sale of the house in Basel to manage.

"I cannot accept that, Master Eamon," I say, shaking my head as my lawyer presents the offer.

He purses his lips as he takes in my defiant gaze. "It is a fair price. Many people are in a position similar to yours. The market is flooded with houses."

I grit my teeth. Clearly, I will have to fight tooth and nail to get a good price on my home.

"Pardon me for disagreeing with you, but not everyone who is returning to England is selling a house. Moreover, my house is in a wonderful location, and we already have renters, assuring the buyer a good income.

Considering everything, I cannot accept this offer." I straighten my back as we stare each other down.

"You may not receive another," he points out.

Smiling, I offer him a cup of sweet mead I prepared myself. "That is a risk I will have to take. But I know the worth of this house. Go back to the buyer and let him know that if he rents out the attic rooms, he can earn an extra twelve pounds per annum. In a few years, the house could pay for itself."

My lawyer closes his folio and gulps down the drink. "Very well, Lady Dorothy. I see you are determined to drive a hard bargain."

It irks me to hear the judgment in his tone.

Doesn't he understand I cannot afford to be pious and show a ladylike demeanour? If I were already wealthy, I could afford to let the house go for less than what it's worth. After all, it's true I am in a rush. However, with five children to look after and an uncertain future, I will fight tooth and nail to get as much as I can.

He goes with a bow and a promise to ask the buyer for more. Since I cannot be there at the negotiating table, I will have to trust him to carry out my wishes.

I watch him go from the window, with a silent prayer that he proves to be an honest man.

After weeks of haggling harder than a merchant, the house is finally sold. The celebration is short-lived as now we have to pack away our belongings and wait.

It's the waiting that is the hardest for me as I tally up the days I have spent away from my country, and family.

During our three-year exile, I have never once allowed myself to feel homesick.

Now all the suppressed emotions wash over me, threatening to drown me in melancholia. Even as the pang in my chest dulls, it never leaves as I move about my day, finally contemplating all the time I lost. I can't wait to see my parents, my siblings, and most of all, my aunt. How had they all changed? What have I missed? Only time will tell.

CHAPTER 2

1559

The sun is high overhead as I step out of the litter. Temporarily blinded by the bright light, I am surprised to be enveloped in the warm embrace of my mother and father.

Their attention turns to my children, who all wait, wide-eyed and well-behaved, with the nursemaid.

Edward performs a little bow to his grandparents, which encourages Elizabeth to dip into a nervous curtsey.

My parents smile kindly upon them and kiss them.

It feels like a dream. I don't even realise I am shedding tears until my mother's thumbs smooth over my cheeks and tut that I will ruin my complexion.

"Let's go inside," she whispers as she takes my hand. "But first I am sure you wish to wash and change out of your clothes."

I nod and look back at my children. "We look like a band of ruffians." My tone is light and adoring.

The six of us are swept up by the waiting servants.

I oversee the children and ensure they're behaving before I let myself be led away. A maid unravels my thick hair, brushing out the tangles and dust as best she can before turning to the soap and water provided in my room.

My mother has ensured I have every luxury brought to me, from oil for my hair to cream for my hands and face.

I pull out a new gown of deep russet from my trunks. As a final touch I wear a string of pearls around my neck.

By the time I emerge from my bedchamber, I am transformed.

"You look splendid," my mother says with an approving nod as she invites me to take a seat by her.

The youngest of my children are tucked away in their beds, tired from the long journey, but Edward and Elizabeth are keen to get to know their English relatives. Three years might not have been long for me, but they have forgotten many things.

My father joins us, three servants carrying trenchers of food and drink following behind him.

Two years ago, Queen Mary accepted my father's petition for the restoration of some of his lands and the title of Baron Stafford. It is a far cry from the dukedom that should be his, but how can we complain when we are little better than beggars?

Despite all my misgivings about the previous queen, I must be grateful to her for allowing this.

The additional income has been enough to improve my parents' lives. I can see it in the smiles on their faces and the thickness of the gown my mother wears. At last, they can afford to be at ease and live in comfort.

They have also been able to make several improvements to the castle. The once-broken wood panels have been replaced, cracks in the walls have been patched, and fires burn in the rooms. A servant lifts the cover on the tray to reveal a marzipan cake. My daughter claps her hands, delighted by the opulent desert.

The dream of being powerful magnates in this land has died. Yet my parents have found joy in the simple comforts of having a pleasant home and food on the table. They are brimming with satisfaction as Edward offers to pour them wine.

"We have sent word to Harry to come. He should be here by tomorrow," my mother says, reaching out to take my hand in hers once more. "We have been apart for far too long."

"I am glad to see you are all well. And the rest of my brothers and sisters too, I suppose?"

My mother nods. "We were able to pay for a proper placard over Margaret's tomb this year. It puts my heart at ease."

I bow my head, saying a silent prayer for my sister who died giving birth to a stillborn daughter.

My mother shuffles in her seat, pulling me out of my thoughts. "In many ways, we have been fortunate to have lost so little when others in my family have suffered," she says.

King Henry VIII's cruelty extended far beyond his wives. My grandmother, the Countess of Salisbury, was maliciously beheaded despite her great age, and her sons with her. Only my uncle living in Rome escaped the king's wrath and suspicion. He returned to England under the reign of Queen Mary only for him to die shortly after she did. Fate has dealt my mother a hard hand, however, she has persevered and now her future looks bright. It's not long before she turns the conversation to lighter matters and inquires about my journey and my children.

"Ursula is a mischief maker. She gives me far more trouble than any other others did at that age," I say.

"She's only three."

"Tell her that," I say with a laugh.

"And now that you are back, what are your plans?" My mother sets aside her empty cup.

"I hoped to speak to my aunt about that. Perhaps there is something that can be done for me."

"Do you wish to remarry?" my mother asks.

I shake my head, avoiding her gaze. "I have other ambitions."

"Positions at court are hard to come by—and expensive," my mother says, guessing my thoughts.

"I can imagine," I say, an edge of stubbornness slipping into my tone. "But it won't stop me from trying. I will write to my stepdaughter. I hear the queen has already offered her a position at court."

"That is a rumour I can confirm. A few days ago, Lady Catherine Knollys was kind enough to write to me. From what I understand, Catherine is now the queen's principal lady of the bedchamber. She could put in a good word for you. After all, in these early days, the queen will be in a generous mood," my mother muses. Considering she's seen three monarchs come and go, I know she's speaking from considerable experience. "Perhaps you will be lucky. Regardless, you and your children will always be welcome here."

"Thank you. Truly," I say, happier than I care to admit that she supports me.

In the days that follow, more reunions take place than I can keep track of. Not all my siblings can make the long journey to see me, but letters stream in, and I am more often at my writing desk than away from it.

My children, who've been apart from family for so long, thrive under the loving attention of two doting grandparents. They are soon joined by more cousins than they can count.

We find our footing as we adjust to our new life. The older children have a tutor, and the younger ones are entertained by nurses. When the weather is good, we go on family picnics and help pick the first cherries of the season. The time is quickly approaching when I will have to leave them in the care of my parents.

Before I go, I arrange little gifts for them. The girls get dolls and new dresses while Edward, being of an age, gets a stout little pony. The gift is meant to be a practical one, but it turns out to create a problem in the household as Elizabeth becomes jealous and I have to cajole Edward into sharing.

"Mother, how can I share with her?" he whines. "She wants to braid its mane and place a crown of flowers on its head. I'll be a laughingstock."

"And who would dare laugh?" I arch an eyebrow. "You should consider yourself above the opinions of others. Edward, if there were more money, I would give you each your own pony. Take out the braids if they bother you so much. I suspect she's doing it to rile you up."

He glares at his sister sewing nearby. She's doing her best to look innocent, but I can tell from the mischievous smile on her face she's pleased with herself.

"Mother," he whines again.

By this point I'm exasperated. "I can always sell the pony if it's going to cause so many problems."

"No," he says. "I'll share."

"Good. I will ask her not to crown the poor thing with flowers. It's important the pony can see where it's going."

Edward looks relieved, and I pat him on the cheek before catching Elizabeth's eye. With a crook of my finger, I summon her to my side. Some days it's like I'm a commander on the battlefield trying to control troops on the verge of desertion. One wrong move on my part and everything will descend into chaos.

～

With peace restored in the nursery, I arrange for a small guard to escort me to Lambeth. My aunt, the Duchess of Norfolk, has her chamberlain escort me to her rooms the moment I arrive.

It's been at least five years since we have seen each other. As I enter the presence chamber, I am shocked by the change I see. She's grown so thin, and deep lines mark her face. I wonder how she can bear the weight of the French hood on her head.

I curtsy low.

"Up you get, Dorothy. We are family, after all." She pretends to scold me though I know she expects decorum to be observed. Then she surprises me by rising swiftly. It seems no one has told her she is now sixty-two and has no business leaping to her feet.

She draws me into an embrace, and I let myself be comforted by her strength and the scent of cloves I've always associated with her. Pulling back, she cradles my face in her palms, and I catch her squinting to get a better look. Elizabeth Stafford will never admit that her sight is failing or that she might find a pair of spectacles useful. Inwardly, I grin at her pride.

"I never thought I'd live to see you step on English soil again," she says, her voice holding the same gravitas it has always had.

"Whereas I never lost hope of being reunited with you. It's been far too long, aunt. I'm happy to see you looking so well."

She grunts and waves away the compliment. "There's no need to flatter me. I've arranged a small feast in your honour. There will be music and enough food to put some meat on your bones. Don't they have food over there in Geneva?" She goes on talking without giving me a chance to answer. The duchess isn't one to be argued with. "After we eat, we shall retire to my bedchamber where we can talk in private."

I hear the warning in her voice. She doesn't want to discuss business now.

The moment I enter the dining hall, I see she has been preparing for my arrival for weeks. It's a mark of her favour that she's gone to all this trouble. So even though I feel awkward I put on a brave face as I am seated at her side at a raised table where everyone can see us. I'm reminded that she keeps to the old traditions, even though now most gentry dine in private apart from their household.

The sound of trumpets announces the start of the meal. Servants bring up food from the kitchens, and I am treated to various dishes of soup, gelatines, and meat lathered in sauce.

As the meal drags on, I feel my aunt examining me. Dabbing the corner of my mouth with a napkin, I turn to face her.

"You are dressed as sombre as a nun. You can't still be in mourning?" she questions.

"No," I admit, self-consciously smoothing a hand over my plain dark skirt. "But it's the fashion."

I say it more to reassure myself than to insult her. My aunt wears a fortune on her back even if the cut is outdated. Tonight, she's chosen a beautiful pale blue gown, elaborately embroidered with Venetian lace and seed pearls.

She sets down her wine and scoffs. "Among the Protestants. They claim it is a sign of piety, but I know it has more to do with poverty. What happened to all the fine jewels and gowns I bought you when you were married?"

I feel my cheeks flush as I study the silver plate from which I've been dining. "They had to be sold, and while I miss them, I don't regret the safety they bought us. I've also heard that the queen prefers women to dress in sombre colours, so perhaps it's for the best."

"You are well informed for an exile," she says. Despite her biting words, her voice is full of tenderness and regret. I know it grates on her that she couldn't find a better match for me, and nothing I say will mollify her guilt.

After she took my sister and me into her household, she had a very public falling out with her husband. In the end, he had her confined in a house far from London, without her own servants and with very little money. Her complaints to the council fell on deaf ears. They certainly wouldn't listen after she'd been caught smuggling letters to Queen Catherine of Aragon—a treasonous act.

Despite all this, life with her was far more interesting than if I stayed home. I suspect I shall be forever grateful to her for the protection and patronage she gave me.

"Did you attend the coronation? I heard it was a grand event," I say.

My aunt looks annoyed I even ask. "Of course, I did."

Then she proceeds to entertain me with a detailed recounting of what everyone wore, the pageants put on by the citizens of London, and finally the ceremony itself.

"The people rejoiced to see her then?" I ask.

"What does that matter? Have you forgotten how they cheered Queen Mary, God rest her soul, when she ascended the throne?"

I'm struck dumb by the harshness in her tone.

She sighs. "It's hard to keep the people's love."

We sit in silence for the rest of the meal. I grow anxious at the prospect of a private audience with her. But there's no backing out now.

CHAPTER 3

Despite the heat my aunt orders her servants to add more logs to the fire burning in her room. We tuck ourselves away in her bedchamber with plenty of mulled ale and sweetmeats. She sits before the roaring fire wrapped in a fur-lined robe while I try to ignore my discomfort.

"You didn't journey all this way merely to see me," my aunt says, once the last of her servants have left. "What do you want?"

"You know that's not true. I've missed you, but I won't insult you by denying that I need your help. Can you help me get a position at court?"

She studies me before adjusting herself in her seat with a grunt. "I suspected as much. Though I wonder why you want to."

It is an invitation to speak, but I find my tongue unco-operative. It is hard to put words to my feelings and desire for recognition and independence.

"Given that I don't wish to marry, serving the queen seems to be the best alternative," I say at last.

"You aren't afraid of the dangers you might find there?"

"I plan on keeping out of trouble. After all, I don't have any lofty ambitions."

My aunt laughs. "Regardless of your intentions, you will be dragged into the muck like all the rest of them. But if it's your wish, I will see what I can do for you." She squints at me, examining my features carefully. "You are pretty but not dazzling, and you are only a few years older than the queen. She will approve of you, I think."

My fingers twist around the chain that hangs around my waist.

"Are you prepared to be separated from your children?" she asks at last.

It is a difficult question to answer. It is common for the nobility to have very little to do with their offspring. I've been fortunate to have my children near me at all times and to be heavily involved in their upbringing.

Could I give that up now? Despite the pang of pain in my heart, I know that I must. The future is so uncertain, and the money I have left won't go far. The last thing I want is to become a burden on my family. My children deserve more, and besides making a grand marriage, the only way for me to accomplish that is to leave them.

"It will be an adjustment. But at court I will be in a position to help them once they are grown. There's nothing else I could offer them."

"You have your bloodline. In these uncertain days," my aunt lets her words trail off. "You never know."

I shake my head in disbelief. "We have no power, wealth or fortune."

"Neither do the Grey sisters, but it doesn't stop the Spanish ambassador from dogging their steps."

"And look what happened because of their ambitions. Their father and oldest sister died. Our own family history is riddled with rebellion and death. How could I forget my grandfather died a traitor? I would be a fool to reach for such heights."

My aunt looks disappointed, but she doesn't give up so easily. "They failed. Who's to say we would as well?"

"This is treasonous talk." I frown.

My aunt shakes her head so fiercely a strand of silver hair escapes her linen coif. "It's reality. The queen is unmarried. There's no clear heir after her death. If we gather enough support, your father could sit on the throne, or your brother after him. You could help them achieve that. Our blood is royal. We have just as much right to the throne as any of the Tudors."

"Queen Elizabeth is young. She will marry and produce an heir for the nation. I would not risk all the safety and support we've gained for a chance at the throne." I ready myself for an outburst, but my aunt merely sinks back into her seat. Has she given up or is she simply retreating? I cannot guess.

"Our family has held the throne before," I add gently, thinking of Anne Boleyn and Kitty Howard. "It didn't end well for them—or for us. Queen Elizabeth has Howard blood in her veins. Why is that not enough?"

"She's a Protestant," my aunt whispers. "She will bring the wrath of God down on England."

"God or the Spanish?" I say with a strained smile.

Her eyes narrow at my impudence, but I'm not seven years old anymore, and I want to put a stop to this dangerous talk.

"Aunt, I am a Protestant too. Do you hate me as well?"

"No, but..." She stops, her brows furrowing as she puzzles out the conundrum I set before her.

Before she has the time to puzzle out her feelings on the subject, I say, "Let's set this discussion aside. It's not worth the risk to even discuss our royal heritage. Can you help me get a place at court or not?"

She turns towards the fire, her features cast in its warm glow. The silence that follows stretches on until I find myself glancing at the clock ticking away on the desk nearby.

Finally, she turns back to me, her lips curled into a mischievous smile. "You'll have your place at court. One way or another."

I place my hand upon the English bible and make a solemn oath to serve the queen and in all things be virtuous, pious and honest. My voice rings out in the silence of the privy chamber. I don't waiver or struggle to recite the words.

Then it's over, and I am swallowed up by the court. Thirty ladies serve the queen, a number greatly reduced from Queen Mary's day. Of course, that doesn't include the groomsmen, ushers, pages, and Yeomen of the Guard on staff.

"She prefers intimacy to grandeur—unless it's a ceremonial or public event. You'll find that the lords are encouraged to leave their wives behind when they visit court," Catherine Knollys explains, as she whisks me past a group of gentlemen standing in the presence chamber. One tries to catch her attention, but she ignores him. I nearly say something, but her hand tightens around mine, and I follow after her.

When we are out of sight, she turns to me and says, "It's best not to engage. They all want one thing from us."

My brow arches, and she laughs.

"They are desperate for news of the queen—or even better if they can get one of us to speak to the queen on their behalf. It's best if you ignore them."

"Even if they offer a very large bribe?"

Catherine Knollys, who served at the court of two queens—Anne of Cleves and Catherine Parr—gives me a sheepish grin. "Well, that's a different story. In such cases, it's best if you use your own judgment. Just be careful..."

I give her a reassuring smile. "I'm not entirely guileless. Don't worry about me. Nor do I think I have any sway with the queen."

"You never know with time. She's generous with her favourites."

Regardless of her reassurances, I cannot help feeling out of place. My childhood and early adult life were not spent wandering around these sumptuous palaces. I've accepted that I'll get lost far more often than I'll care to admit. As we walk, Catherine goes over the various protocols and customs at court. Despite receiving an education befitting someone of my rank, these are still new to me. For the first time since I set out to do this, I feel daunted by what's ahead of me.

She takes me to all the places I might need to know. The jewel house and the queen's wardrobe are kept in an entirely separate palace, but they store a few items at court wherever we go. At any time of day, the queen might ask for something, and it is the duty of a lady-in-waiting to fetch it for her.

It's strange that our roles are reversed now. Where once I was her stepmother, now I am her student. But Catherine Knollys is more than happy to take me under her wing, and I never show an ounce of ingratitude.

"The queen will be returning from the hunt. If the weather is good, she is often outdoors until dinner at noon. Most of the time, we join her."

Wringing my hands nervously, I say, "I haven't purchased a horse yet. I was hoping to wait until I receive my salary."

"Don't worry. You may borrow one from the queen's stable. She keeps several horses for her ladies and guests to ride. Robert Dudley has been made Master of the

Horse and he's quite passionate about his stock. You won't find any tired old nags that can't keep up among the queen's horses."

Somewhat relieved, I nod. "I've heard of him. I am surprised to find him so honoured."

Catherine's expression darkens for an imperceptible moment before it returns to her usual calm. "I daresay you will understand much when you meet him at last."

At the very end of the tour, she takes me to see my assigned room. In the secluded privacy, she takes a step back to admire my new dress. The heavy black damask is embroidered with a hem of gold silk embroidered with a blackwork pattern. I wear a string of pearls at my neck, and my French hood, gifted to me by my mother, is inlaid with pearls stitched together in a floral pattern.

"You've come prepared." She nods approvingly. "The queen prefers us to wear black or white at all times. Fashionable cuts and luxurious fabrics, but nothing that will make us stand out."

I raise an eyebrow.

"Everything is a play," she explains, adjusting her own full skirts. "We must never outshine her."

I can understand that. Queen Elizabeth is new to her throne, untested and untried. She must ensure she always captures the attention and respect of the people who serve her and visit court.

"There is a lot of pomp and ceremony, but the court is never short of entertainment." Catherine opens the lid of my trunk and rifles through the four other gowns I brought with me, along with petticoats, linen shifts and coifs, and another headdress. "You may wish to purchase larger ruffs. These are rather small."

I was thinking of my comfort, but I make a note to write to my mother.

With the tour of the palace complete, Catherine helps me change into a new gown and we return to the privy chamber to await the queen. I draw the attention of many who glance my way. Those who know I am the new lady-in-waiting wonder how much I've paid for the privilege, while others look on with jealousy that their candidate was not accepted.

Before the queen returns, I take a cursory glance at myself to make sure I look acceptable. My black silk gown was made from material borrowed from my mother's storerooms. Parts of it were borrowed from her old gowns and altered to fit the latest fashion. The frontlet is a beautiful cream, embroidered with lacework I tatted myself in Geneva. It's a modest yet rich gown I believe is suitable.

Catherine invites me to sit with her as she fusses over a painted screen.

"This has been stained with something." She points to a patch near the bottom. "Wine, no doubt."

"It can be repainted, can it not?"

"Yes." She lets out a heavy sigh. "But it should've been taken away. The queen is very attentive to such things, and we, being older, will be blamed." I must look puzzled, because she explains. "The younger ladies are immature and wild. They will make a mess, and rather than clean up or fix their mistake, they will leave it. Were we ever so badly behaved?"

"Certainly. We've simply forgotten now that we've grown old," I joke.

"Old? You certainly cannot be?" says a male voice, gruff and masculine. Embarrassed, I turn around to find a formidable gentleman in a padded jacket, with the most ostentatious white ostrich feather sticking out of his hat.

"Sir Nicholas Bacon," Catherine, says, getting to her feet and performing a curtsey. "May I present to you Lady Dorothy Stafford."

"Ah, the new addition," he says, bowing to me as I curtsey to him. I cannot help the flush in my cheeks.

"You are Lord Keeper, or am I mistaken?" I say, trying to cover up my ignorance.

"I am, Lady Dorothy. The queen is on her way," he says, a twinkle of mischief in his expression. "I find it's best to avoid topics of age. Some ladies are more sensitive than yourself."

I blanch, realising he is referring to the queen. "Thank you, sir."

It's not long before he's proven to be correct. The queen enters her privy chamber with little pomp, yet everyone stops in their tracks. Her very presence is enough to capture your attention.

We all bow until she invites us to rise.

At last, I can get a good look at her. She's tall and slim, and the gauzy wired wings that frame her face are wider than her hips, yet she carries herself with grace and strength. The gown she wears is a tawny brown, embroidered with motifs of hunting dogs baying at deer set in a forest. Even from afar, I can make out the emerald green gems sewn into the leaves of the trees.

She approaches Catherine Knollys, removing her gloves and handing them to her. "See that these are put somewhere safe. They are precious to me."

I steal a glance at them, admiring the beautifully embroidered ferns on the hem of the beige kit leather.

Noticing the silence, I look up to find her watching me. Her piercing gaze is unnerving as she takes me in. Then her dark eyes travel to the amethyst brooch pinned to my frontlet. She must recognise the Howard heirloom on loan from my aunt because she gives me a tight smile.

"And you must be my cousin, Lady Dorothy."

I curtsey. "Yes, Your Majesty."

"How lovely to have another member of my family at court," she says.

I cannot make out from her tone whether she is being sarcastic.

As she turns to her left, a tall man steps forward to listen. "Sir Robert, in the brief span of a few months I've gone from being an orphan ignored by all to being smothered by the loving attention of my family."

"Extended family, Your Grace," he says, not even bothering to glance my way. "Though we all pray that those of your blood shall indeed surround you."

"Robert, what are you saying?"

He prostrates himself before her as if he were an actor in a play. "It is merely the desire of all your subjects that one day you will create a small army of princes and princesses that resemble you, though,"—he pauses for a heavy dramatic sigh— "they cannot come close to perfection, being mere copies of the original."

The queen is amused, so I have to bite the inside of my cheek to keep from gasping at his forwardness. Clearly, this is commonplace.

Queen Elizabeth swats him on the shoulder with her fan in a mocking reprimand. "Rise, Sir Robert. You should know better than to speak to me of children."

"I cannot help it. Your presence inspires me to think of such things, Your Grace," he says, getting to his feet. His deep brown eyes are full of meaning as he regards her. It's clear to everyone in the room that he's in love with her, and judging by the way she looks at him the feeling is mutual.

I keep my expression bland as I meet my stepdaughter's eye. She gives me a nearly imperceptible nod. This is what she was alluding to earlier.

I regard the proprietary way Sir Robert holds the queen's hand as he helps her to her seat. Sir Nicholas Bacon steps forward with his petition, weighing the chances the queen will be upset if he disturbs them now. It's Robert Dudley who invites him to approach the queen.

The queen should put him in his place for subverting her authority, but she does not.

I'm not the only one who frowns at this. While I cannot claim to be a skilled politician, I know that if this continues, it'll spell disaster for her. Even if Robert Dudley were free to marry—which he is not, he's been married these last seven years—he's a highly improper choice.

Besides his good looks and confident bearing, he has nothing—not even gold—to offer her. What lies did he spin to make the queen forget he helped his father overturn the line of succession in order to put Queen Jane on the throne? The plot failed, but he's shown he's a traitor to the crown, just like his father and grandfather before him. If Queen Elizabeth ever honours him with the title of King Consort, it will incite outrage and even rebellion in the kingdom.

On that I would stake my life.

CHAPTER 4

The creak of wood and metal wake me. I hadn't even realised I dozed off by the fire. The logs are nothing but glowing hot embers now. Forcing myself to be alert, I look towards the queen's bedchamber just as Mary Sidney pokes her head out.

"Yes?" I say, attempting to rub the sleep from my eyes.

"The queen wishes to speak to Sir William Cecil immediately," Mary whispers with a wary look over her shoulder, as if she's afraid the queen will pop up behind her with some new demand.

I glance at the clock. It's nearly midnight.

"Of course." I stand.

"Will you be all right?" she asks. A flash of annoyance crosses her features as she stares at me poignantly. Irritation flares within me. It's as though I can hear her wondering if I will get lost or be too slow in fetching him.

I purse my lips. It's been a few weeks since I've come to court. Her concern would be touching if I didn't know how she and the other ladies call me a country bumpkin behind my back. We are a competitive lot.

Not deigning to answer her, I say, "I'll be back as soon as possible with the private secretary."

She gives me a curt nod, and I hurry out.

It's easier to navigate the hallways and stairs in the loose gown I've changed into. There's no farthingale to contend with, but the unexpected chill of the palace has me gritting my teeth to keep from chattering. I clutch the furred neckline of the gown tight against my throat, but there's nothing I can do about the slashed sleeves that let the cold seep through the thin linen shift beneath. I make a mental note to sew a pair of new sleeves for this gown in the future as I make my way to the secretaries' apartments.

I knock once. No one answers. After a few more seconds go by, I knock again, more insistently than before.

Finally, the door opens and a drowsy pageboy answers. He looks alarmed to find me there and performs a clumsy bow.

"How may I help you, lady?"

"Her majesty wishes to see Sir William. Please inform—"

"I'm here," a voice interrupts from the darkened room.

I hear the shuffle of heavy fabric.

"Stop fussing," the voice says again.

An oil lamp is lit, and a serious man dressed in black robes pushes the pageboy out of the way. William Cecil looks like he just rolled out of bed. The strings of his cap have been hastily tied under his chin and sit askew. I see his valet fretting over his master's appearance, but he is too busy thinking. His eyes dart from me to the page as he rubs a hand over his beard. "This will be about the Scottish ambassador's arrival or the Flemish trade..." He trails off when I offer no assistance and clears his throat. "Well, we cannot keep her grace waiting. John, grab your writing desk. Wait. On second thought, I doubt she'll want you inside with me. Tom, with me."

The pageboy he'd pushed out of the way bounds forward holding an oil lamp precariously in one hand.

The three of us take off for the queen's apartments with me. For the Yeomen of the Guard stationed outside the queen's rooms, these late-night meetings have grown commonplace. They take one look at me and nod us through.

I knock on her bedroom door, and Cecil is invited in while the rest of us are left out in the privy chamber. Mary Sidney joins me as I warm my hands by the dying fire.

"Will they be long?"

She shrugs. "It varies. Sometimes it's only a matter of minutes, but it could be hours."

Pulling back my sleeve, I grab a log from the basket nearby and add it to the fire. Then I use the poker to stoke the flames high. I can feel her watching me from the corner of my eye. Is this beneath someone of my station? Probably. But I'm far more certain she appreciates the warmth. One thing I'm not afraid of doing is getting my hands dirty.

Setting the poker back in its place, I pull a stool forward and settle down on it. Mary still hangs back, watching me curiously.

"I've seen the Duchess of Norfolk roast chestnuts herself. I'd rather be warm than call for a scullery maid to come build up the fire."

Mary is amused by this piece of information and pulls up a chair beside me. "Did she really? I cannot imagine it. She came to court for the coronation—a serious and formidable figure if I ever saw one."

"Yes. She thought her maid was doing it wrong." I smile at the childhood memory.

A long silence follows, but I keep hearing shuffling behind us. The pageboy cannot stand still.

"Tom, why don't you pour us a glass of ale from that cupboard over there?" I ask.

Happy for the distraction, he bounds towards the cupboard and comes forward with a tray. The oil lamp has been abandoned on the floor, and I feel compelled to scold him.

"Thank you, Tom. but you should know better than to leave a lit lamp like that on the floor. One spill and this entire room will go up in flames."

He blanches, his body quivering as he rushes back to pick up the lamp, which nearly results in him dropping it.

"Seriously, I'm starting to suspect you are an assassin," I say, unable to help my irritation. He can't be more than eighteen. But even so, his ineptitude is shocking.

Mary hides a smile as she takes a deep drink of her wine.

"Please, pardon me, my lady. My father..."

"Got you this position, didn't he?"

"Yes. But I keep making a mess of everything. I don't mean to make so many mistakes," he says, hanging his head low.

"Well, my advice to you would be to slow down and focus on every task. You'll find you are less likely to make mistakes that way."

He gives a solemn nod, and I hope he will take my advice to heart.

"You are rather brave speaking to Cecil's eldest child like that," Mary whispers to me.

I feel nausea gathering at the back of my throat, but outwardly I show no regret. I stand by what I said, though I might have tempered my words had I known who he was.

"In appearance and temperament, he doesn't take after his father at all," I say, staring at the gangly youth.

"No. Takes after his mother, I suppose. I doubt he will make a good courtier. His father is disappointed. He's the only surviving issue from Cecil's first marriage. But his new wife has already given him two sons. Perhaps the other children will have a knack for it," Mary Sidney offers freely.

"Or he may surprise everyone," I offer, though as I

watch Tom shift his weight from one foot to the other, I find myself highly uncertain.

At last Cecil emerges from the queen's bedchamber. He looks haggard, but that's hardly surprising given that it's nearly two in the morning. He bows his head to us and motions for his son to follow him out.

"Well, let's hope she falls asleep," Mary whispers. "I'm so tired. The minute my eyes close, I'll drift off to sleep."

Feeling the same, I give her a strained smile. Even words are hard to come by this late at night.

At dawn, maids of the queen's household wake us and help us dress. It is an affair that takes the better part of an hour as layer after layer is attached. Countless pins keep our finery in place. I start to feel more like a pincushion than a woman. Once we are ready we go to her majesty's bedchamber, where she has washed and changed into a fresh linen shift. Then, it is our turn to help her dress.

Today she will be meeting with a German dignitary, here to discuss trade and request help with the continuing war against the Spanish. To honour him, the queen has commanded a selection of jewels from the German provinces to be brought out of the treasury. After much debate she selects a gold brooch in the shape of a walled city inlaid with pearls. When pinned to her russet gown, it draws your eye.

I step forward to brush her hair. The queen prefers to

wear her hair loose, or wearing velvet hats to allow her to show off its beautiful colour and length. The Germans are known for their propriety, so she forgoes this habit of hers. When I am done another set of hands plaits it so it may fit under a matching French hood.

The whole ensemble has taken us an hour to put on. Next we paint her face with light cream made from crushed eggshells, alum, and other ingredients known to illuminate the face.

At last the Queen is ready, and she examines herself in the full-length mirror with a smile, appreciating our hard work.

"The weather is lovely outside, is it not?"

"Yes, Your Majesty," a lady says, nodding.

"Good. We shall walk around the rose gardens this morning before my meeting."

I hear some groans from the back of the room.

The queen's eyes flash. "Exercise is as good for the soul as it is for the mind," she admonishes us.

Even I, who was always an active person, find it hard to keep up with her fast pace, so I'm not paying attention when she looks back and requests that I walk beside her.

Being singled out like this is a great honour. The other ladies fall back so we might have the illusion of privacy. I have no idea what I did to earn this show of favour, so I wait for her to speak first.

"You've spent some time in Germany, as I understand it," the queen says.

"Yes, only a few months before moving to Geneva, Your Grace," I say.

"You speak the language?"

"A little."

"Is that modesty or honesty?"

"Honesty, Your Grace. I haven't spent enough time studying the language to declare myself fluent in it."

She hums, tapping her long fingers on the boning of her frontlet. "Nonetheless, I would like you at my side during today's audience."

"It would be an honour, Your Grace."

"I don't forget how well you've served me since coming to court," she says. "You seem to be a helpful sort of woman. I hope you will serve me well in the future."

"Thank you." I tilt my head, hiding my reddening cheeks.

"I am plagued by people seeking something from me. It's refreshing to see someone who is more interested in serving me than getting a reward."

"Your majesty, I am just like any other. I cannot claim I do not serve you for selfish reasons."

"And what might those selfish reasons be?" Her eyes spark, amused.

"For the glory of being in your presence."

She laughs. "Well spoken."

Our tête-à-tête has come to an end, but she doesn't send me away from her side. Now might be my chance to ask if I can go visit my children, but I dare not ask yet.

Half-way through our walk, we are joined by Robert Dudley, and I fall back as they begin to talk about some upcoming tournament he's arranging in her honour.

As I return to my place in the line of ladies, I pass by

Lady Katherine Grey, who is whispering to her friend, Jane Seymour. Their eyes skim over me and then they giggle as they catch me watching them.

The young ladies are my junior by over a decade. I will not allow them to bully me as if we were children together in the nursery. Just as I'm about to reprimand them, I hesitate. Katherine Grey outranks me. By all accounts, she might be the next in line for the throne. It would not be smart of me to invite more trouble or cause a scene.

Little by little, I stop being the ignorant newcomer. It helps that I don't let myself get pulled into petty gossip and rivalries with the other ladies. I perform my duties without complaint and am always ready to lend a helping hand to any who need it.

It's only the younger maids who seem persistent in teasing me and snubbing me. Lady Jane Seymour and her bosom friend Katherine Grey are happy to giggle at my attempts to learn a courtly dance.

They were raised at court their whole lives. Their education was far different from my own. There was never a shortage of dance masters. The subtle courtly manners became ingrained in them from an early age. These flourishes don't come as easily to me, and I cannot deny that it stings my pride. What I cannot help but wonder is how either of them could have such inflated egos given that both their fathers died as traitors on the block. Katherine Grey even saw her sister, Lady Jane Grey, who many already regard as a martyr, die for her faith.

I see how the queen's sharp gaze drifts to the young girl. Her eyes are full of disdain, as if like me, she would rather not have the Grey sisters here at court at all. But the royal blood that flows in her veins means she cannot allow them to leave her sight.

As marriage negotiations for the Queen pour in but continue to go unanswered, many look at Katherine Grey as the next logical heir to the English throne. There is, of course, Mary Stuart, daughter of King James, nephew to Henry VIII through his sister Margaret Tudor, married to the Scottish King. But in the Act of Succession, Henry VIII declared that his sister Margaret's heirs could not inherit the English throne. The Protestants of the realm can breathe a sigh of relief, for Queen Mary of Scots has been married to the Dauphin of France, meaning she is as Catholic as they come.

After the former Queen Mary, no one wants another Catholic on the throne, especially not one married to France. It rankles the English people's pride to think that England might be swallowed up by the French Empire.

Despite all this, I am certain that some in the Kingdom support her claim. In truth, many of us are worried that the French might invade. King Charles of France has certainly made threats. Loyal Englishmen and women say a prayer every night that the Spanish will keep the French army occupied so they can't turn their attention on England.

Given the uneasy state of the realm, it's no wonder the Queen's councillors wish to settle the line of succession one way or another.

"We shall invite him to court," Cecil says, his tone firm.

The queen is breaking her fast after attending matins. I fill her goblet with watered-down wine as she peers at Cecil. "I don't feel it's necessary to even entertain the proposal. He's as Catholic as they come. I shall not have him as my consort. It would be like inviting a viper into my bed."

"Your majesty, an alliance with the Holy Roman Empire would cement your own safety and put a stop to the French ambitions."

"I rule by divine right. The French are overreaching—"

"It doesn't matter," Cecil interrupts. He checks himself. "Your majesty, I know, as does every loyal subject in this realm, that you are the rightful ruler of England, but at the moment we are alone, friendless, without any allies to stand against the might of Spain or France. And God forbid if they should decide to work together."

I have to admire the cool, collected picture the queen presents to her frantic councillor as she goes on sipping her wine.

"King Philip has promised to be my dearest friend, even though I have rejected his marriage proposal," she says with some mirth. "Are you saying that he would move against me so soon?"

I catch the sarcasm in the queen's tone, but from the way Cecil's eyes have gone wide, he hasn't. At a loss for what to say, he flounders.

Robert Dudley chooses that moment to stride into the privy chamber, filled with boundless energy and excitement. "Your majesty," he greets her with a deep bow and smile. "I have good news. A rowing regatta has been arranged for your entertainment, and the city of London is providing fireworks to for the feast of Saint Edward the Confessor."

"Thank you for letting me know, Sir Robert. Will you not have something to eat?" She invites him to her table.

He approaches but does not sit. Robert accepts a goblet of wine, which he drinks down in one gulp. It's as if Cecil has disappeared from the room entirely. The queen's private secretary shows every sign of displeasure, from the curl of his lip to the narrowing of his eyes, as he regards Dudley being shown such favouritism.

"It is good to have a friend at my side," the queen says, her hand touching the padding of his slashed sleeves. "You find me harassed by marriage proposals this morning."

"Who is it now?" He sits on a stool close to her but not so close that the cloth of estate hangs over his head. He might be brazen, but even he has his limits.

"The Archduke Charles," Cecil says. "As I was trying to explain to the queen, it's an excellent match, and with it, we would win an alliance with the Holy Roman Empire."

Dudley sniffs as if he's smelled something displeasing. "Is that the best they can do? He's nothing but a boy, and a Catholic one at that."

Cecil frowns at the rudeness but says nothing as the queen laughs.

"Is he really?" she leans in towards Robert, who whispers something in her ear that sets her laughing again.

"Your majesty, he is not much younger than yourself. I have been assured by the ambassador that he is handsome, virile, and strong. The emperor has suggested that if we gave the archduke permission to practise the Catholic faith in private, he would outwardly conform to the English Church."

"What message would that send my people?" The queen shakes her head.

"This would be a minor concession in the grander scheme of things, Your Grace," Cecil says. Robert snorts with derision, and Cecil can barely hold back from snapping at him.

These two councillors should be working together, but as far as I can tell they are at each other's throats more often than not. I wonder what game Robert Dudley is playing at, but clearly his support of the queen is winning him her favour.

"All I am suggesting is that you allow the ambassador an audience so you can formally receive the proposal."

Queen Elizabeth holds out her goblet and I refill it,

finding it hard to keep my hand steady amid such tense discussions.

For a moment, her eyes flick to me and gives me a small smile, as if she can read my thoughts.

"Arrange a meeting with him, then. But Cecil, I make no promises other than to hear him out. You must not make any on my behalf. I do not want them to accuse me of being changeable. My word when given is not given lightly. I will never break it."

He is quick to bow low, but I catch the twitch in his lips. Of all the games Queen Elizabeth enjoys playing, her favourite is keeping her councillors on their toes. It might be true that once she makes a promise, she doesn't falter—but she rarely makes promises. Her privy councillors have learned that decisions she's made in the morning may alter by nightfall. They must act faster than her changeable nature.

"Thank you, Your Majesty. I shall leave you to enjoy your breakfast." He glances towards Dudley, reserving his ire for the man he deems responsible for the queen refusing to marry.

I watch him retreat from the chamber, never once turning his back on his sovereign. I feel pity for him.

"Shall I play the lute for you, Your Majesty?" Robert asks, eyes twinkling mischievously. "I have composed a new song this morning, just for you."

"I would love to hear it, my sweet Robin."

One of her ladies comes forward with a lute. Robert takes it with a cheeky grin that has the woman blushing red. He's content to flirt with every handsome lady he comes across. Soon his deep baritone voice fills the chamber. Even I can't help but admire his skill. He certainly has the tools to woo anyone. His eyes lock on to the Queen's as he sings of love and unending devotion.

I feel a pang of longing. While my marriage was happy enough, the passion wasn't there. Watching the two of them makes me wish things had been different.

CHAPTER 5

I 'm rushing back with a note for the queen when two laundresses come giggling around the corner and we bump into each other.

"Pardon, milady," one says with a small curtsey.

My head is pounding from a combination of too much wine and reading by candlelight late into the night.

I'm tempted to wave them on their way when I get a good look at their faces.

"Wait," I say, just as they are almost out of sight. They turn as one, their good humour melting away. It sets me on high alert as I regard their basket full of linen sheets.

I jump straight to the question. "Are those the queen's bed sheets?"

They are unwilling to answer, sly smiles appear on their faces. I know this game. I've played it many times before. My hand dips in the pocket of my dress, and I pull out two coins.

I get my answer as soon as I hand over the coins.

"They are."

"And what is so funny about them that has you giggling like this?"

The one on the left arches an eyebrow mocking me. "Why do you assume it's about the sheets, milady?"

My lips purse. "Because everything is about the queen. Shall I send you to Sir Francis for questioning?"

They go pale at the mention of the queen's spymaster. In their fear, they even look over their shoulders.

"The Spanish ambassador cornered us as we left her rooms, inquiring about the state of her bedsheets."

"And he paid you handsomely, I'm sure. So what did you tell him?" I take a threatening step forward.

"Nothing important." Her voice is squeaky.

"He must've been pleased by the information. Why else would you be in such high spirits that you are giggling down the halls? What did you tell him?" I ask, rubbing at my temples.

"We said the sheets weren't stained this morning, and we'd found them rumpled."

"That is all?"

They look down at their toes. "She had just risen out of bed when we came in. Lord Robert Dudley was there."

I hold back a curse. It looks bad. The Spanish ambassador won't care if he came in this morning. All he will care about is that it looked like the queen had invited him to her bed. That he might have spent the night alone with her. The queen has no shame about letting him see her in her stays and petticoat, but they are never alone. She guards her reputation closely.

"You will tell no one else what you may or may not have seen. The queen slept poorly last night. She did indeed toss and turn, but not because she was with a man, rather that she carries the burden of her country on her shoulders. Such idle gossip is enough to send anyone to prison. Do you understand?"

They gulp, nodding their heads.

"Should anyone ask you, please don't forget to mention that she also sleeps with two of her lady's maids in her room each night. I will take those baskets."

"Milady?"

"It's an order. Be glad I'm saving you from far worse punishment." I soften my tone. "I love the queen far too much to wish to see harm come to her.

"Of course. We are honoured to serve her too. Every day we pray for her safety."

I fight the urge to roll my eyes. If that were true, they wouldn't be tempted by a few coins to divulge secrets and gossip that would undermine the queen's reputation. But if life has taught me anything, it's that love and loyalty are not one and the same. I cannot hate them or curse them, for am I not at court doing the same thing? They grow anxious in the prolonged silence.

"I'm happy to hear that. You are dismissed."

They set down their baskets and scurry down the hall. My shoulders slump as I consider the mess I've put myself in. I stack the baskets one on top of the other.

They are heavy, but my years in Geneva where I bore the brunt of the housework are put to good use.

When I stopped them, I did not know what my plan was going to be. But I couldn't trust those maids not to sell the sheets. I can only imagine how thrilled the Spanish would be for the chance to display the sheets upon which the Queen of England has debased herself. I shudder at the thought.

I'm so lost in my thoughts and the effort of holding my baskets that I nearly walk into someone. I rush to apologise.

"No harm done," he says, then he takes me in. "I had no idea that the laundresses were so well dressed these days."

I adjust my grip on the baskets, the pain of holding on to the handles growing unbearable, but I don't want to set them down either. Not with Sir William Pickering looking at me with amusement in his deep blue eyes.

I straighten. "I am no laundress..."

He sweeps me a courteous bow. "I know who you are, my lady. I am simply amused to find you here carrying a basket of linen."

My hand cramps, and I lose my precarious hold on the baskets. I lean forward, trying to adjust my grip but instead find myself falling. Sir William Pickering, unencumbered, steps forward, catching me with one hand while steadying the baskets with another before they can spill their contents all over the floor.

I take a deep breath, first from the shock and then his

closeness. I admire the intricately embroidered gloves he wears—a blue pansy in a field of wheat.

"Do you like them?" his voice is a whisper.

I flush, pulling away. "They are very well made, which is why I'm sure you bought them in the first place, is it not?"

His lips curl into a smile. Leaning down, he picks up the baskets without shame.

For a moment, I hesitate. "What are you doing?"

"Helping you, is that not obvious?"

"I want to ask why, but I fear then you will accuse me of being ungracious."

"Where to, my lady?"

"The queen's rooms. I will ask Lady Kat Ashley for help."

"I suppose asking the servants for help would be out of the question?"

"Quite so." I don't feel like allowing him into my confidence. I've seen him around the court. His straightforward manner has won him many friends, and the queen likes him, but he has no reason to be so friendly with me unless he wants something. I consider myself forewarned. When I was younger and more ignorant about the ways of the world, I might have been blushing right now and half in love with a man like Pickering.

We reach the back entrance, and I usher him in as he remains stubborn about relinquishing his hold on the baskets.

"If you merely wanted to gain entrance to the Queen's private chambers, you might have asked me."

"And you might have said no," he says with a wink. "It was faster this way."

Ah. There it is—the reason why he was willing to be so gallant.

If the ladies weren't busy preparing to attend Mass, then we might have drawn a lot of attention to us. I lead the way, weaving my way around them towards Kat Ashley.

She looks surprised to see me and Pickering. Even more at what he's carrying.

"What is the meaning of this?"

"Laundresses were claiming unsavoury things about her majesty, and I confiscated what the sheets as they would no doubt have used them as proof, real or imagined."

"And I was merely trying to assist a lady in need," Pickering says.

Kat Ashley looks unimpressed by his pluck. Pinching the bridge of her nose, she turns to me. "You've done well. I shall be sure to inform Cecil about this, and her majesty should be told too." She pauses. "They may wish to know the details of these rumours."

I swallow hard, feeling the heat rise to my cheeks. "I am at their disposal."

"You may leave the linens with me. I'll deal with it."

"Thank you."

I curtsey, and when I turn around, I find that Sir William hasn't left my side. My brow arches in silent question. "You've helped me with my heavy burden. What business do you have with me? Can I help you with something?" Everything is a transaction at court, so I am surprised when he shakes his head. His eyes twinkle with mischief.

"No, fair lady, I need nothing from you, but I would ask that you look upon me more kindly in the future."

My expression is impassive, though I'm fighting back a smile.

In the early days of the queen's ascension, he had put himself forward as a potential suitor for her. He might only be a knight, but during diplomatic missions abroad he amassed a fortune that could've tempted the queen. His charm and wit only added to his chances. However, it all went to his head, and he ruined his prospects by dressing and acting overly grand. The queen never banished him from her side, but neither has she invited him into her private confidence again. Especially not with Robert Dudley playing court to her.

Maybe Pickering sees me as an easy target he can win over by flirting with me. After all, I am new to court. Cautiously, I don't give him an answer and eventually he leaves this private inner sanctum.

"I'm sorry, spirit," Queen Elizabeth says to a despondent Cecil as he brings her the news that the marriage talks with the archduke have been kindly rejected.

We are dressing her for a celebratory feast in her honour.

I help Mary Sidney tie the sleeves of her majesty's

gown in place. They are Italian, made from a brilliant white velvet that shimmers in the candlelight. A diamond pattern, hemmed by gold braid, is cut into the cloth to reveal the red silk beneath. With great speed and deftness, I pull the red silk of the sleeves beneath through the openings. Even though she isn't fully dressed, the effect is already striking.

There is no doubt in my mind that no one will be able to take their eyes off her.

My task finished, I curtsey and move out of the way so the next lady can come forward with the frontlet. The jewelled piece is decorated with seed pearls. A ruby brooch will be pinned to the top, and a girdle of rubies, currently being examined by Blanche Parry, will complete the white and red ensemble.

The queen will be the embodiment of purity and virginity—something the courtiers and foreign dignitaries present today will surely notice. It won't be long before the news that she's rejected the archduke's suit will be known. We all wonder who will be enticed to come forward next?

The Spanish have been bristling. Negotiations with Phillip broke down long ago, and though he wasn't eager to see Elizabeth married to the archduke, he preferred that match to the one now put on the table.

"It is for the best," Elizabeth says again to Cecil as he finishes reading out the emperor's letter espousing his regret. "I've heard that the archduke is more pious than was initially reported and would be unwilling to attend our English services. He has also refused to travel to

England to meet with me. How could he expect me to agree to a marriage based on a portrait alone?"

Cecil's lips purse. "That is the way of royal marriages. He was insulted we even asked."

She laughs. "You see, spirit, he is not the man for me. He would not stand being governed by a woman. We would come to hate one another."

Cecil looks away so she won't see the look of frustration on his face. We all know how he feels about the subject. To him, as to many men, a woman on the throne of England subverts the natural order of the world. He chafes at the bit like an irritated horse, but Queen Elizabeth, for all her faults, keeps her hands firmly on the reins. Despite this, she is a monarch who values the opinions of her advisors.

My stomach has been upset all morning, and I take a turn around the gardens, enjoying the fresh air and the fragrant smell of flowers, when I hear loud giggling and raised voices.

The knot garden is a maze of twists and turns. Some hedges tower over me. I wonder who has snuck away to meet with some lover. Certainly I hope it isn't one of the queen's maids. Walking towards the sound, I find I've come across a group of the queen's maids. Among them, I see Lady Katherine Grey, who was given leave to visit her ailing mother. They are watching her tiny marmoset monkey perform a little trick, clapping and laughing as it plays with a ribbon. But my eyes are drawn away from this childish play to the unmistakable figure of the Spanish ambassador.

He is the first to see me as well. Respectfully, he inclines his head towards me and then, with a word to Katherine Grey retreats down the other way.

"Come join us, Lady Dorothy. There's no need to watch us from the shadows," she calls out to me.

"You are mistaken," I say, coming forward, feeling more like a schoolmaster than ever. "I was merely walking by. But what I cannot understand is why you are out here and not with the queen."

"We were just taking a stroll around the garden for some fresh air," Lady Jane says, having the decency to look abashed.

"How is your mother? You pleaded with the queen to let you go visit her. Yet I find you frolicking in the garden, as light-hearted as a lark."

"My mother is doing poorly."

I arch an eyebrow. The girl will never be a politician. "Then I'm even more surprised to find you laughing and playing here."

She gapes at me. "I am doing nothing wrong."

"And the Spanish ambassador? What did he have to say to you?"

"He—" she says, before clamping her mouth shut. At last she realises how this must look. "This wasn't a meeting. De Feria was kind enough to ask how I am faring. He is very attentive."

Jane Seymour grabs her hand. I catch her giving her friend's hand a tight squeeze.

"Do you find the court an unfriendly place, Lady Katherine? Are you miserable here?"

"Of course not," she snaps, losing her temper. "I meant about my mother. He was consoling me about my mother's illness and said he would pray for her quick recovery."

"I suggest you all return to the queen's apartments. It looks suspicious that all of you are gathered out here, surrounded by admirers and even foreign dignitaries. Surely, anything the Spanish ambassador has to say to you could be said in front of her majesty."

Katherine's eyes regard me coolly. There's something imperious about the way she looks at me, and I know before she speaks she's about to make a grave mistake.

"Queen Elizabeth must always be at the centre of everything. She wouldn't countenance anyone paying any special attention to me or anyone else."

"She is the queen," I say, stressing every word. Katherine doesn't hear the warning. It's no wonder given how inflated her ego has grown in the last few weeks.

"My poor sister Jane was queen too. She never ignored us. Even Queen Mary took the time to speak to us and was never—"

Jane Seymour interrupts her. "Lady Dorothy, she is distressed. Her mother is doing poorly. She doesn't know what she is saying."

I straighten, smoothing a hand over my skirts. "I understand." My gaze flicks to the distraught Katherine, whose words could amount to treason. "I am sorry for your troubles. Truly I am."

With that, I turn and head back the way I can.

I don't make it far before Katherine runs towards me, catching up to me and taking my hand in hers. I turn to regard her. Has it sunk in what she has said?

"You will not gossip about me," she says. "You tricked me into saying terrible things."

I peer behind her to her seven other friends. "I don't think I did. There are plenty of witnesses to our conversation."

"They would never betray me," she whispers, eyes wide with fright.

I feel a pang of pity for her. She truly learned nothing from her sister's downfall. "Your own father provided evidence against his own daughter and your sister, Lady Jane Grey, in court. Do you think these ladies would be more loyal? Perhaps you meant no harm, but your words are treasonous. You must learn to curb your tongue."

"I will," she swears.

I pull my hand out of her grip.

"You won't repeat what I said, right?" The desperation in her voice is great. "Only. I don't wish to make the queen upset with me. She was so kind, letting me visit my sick mother." She bats her lashes.

I say nothing as I walk away, ignoring her calling after me, even as she lets out an undignified shriek.

Uncertainty twists in my gut by the time I've returned to the queen's apartments. There no way I would keep such an important conversation from the queen and her councillors. However, I don't want to be the means of destroying a young woman who is too foolish and quick with her words.

I pull Catherine Knollys away from her work, and we speak in an alcove. She is far closer to the queen than I am. She will know how to tackle this delicate matter.

"You must inform Sir Walsingham. I will speak to the queen myself when the time is right. But we cannot keep this from her. Lady Katherine Grey is no idle gossip, and if the Spanish ambassador is finding ways to meet with her—well, this is serious."

I nod.

CHAPTER 6

Sir Francis Walsingham meets with me after dinner. Our conversation is brief as he's already caught wind of the Spanish ambassador's movements.

"I don't know what was said between Lady Katherine Grey and the ambassador. He left shortly after I arrived."

"Do you think they planned to meet there?" he asks.

"You'd be the better judge of that, sir." I doubt much happens in England that he doesn't know about.

"I would like to know your opinion." He presses.

What do I say? I don't want to be the one held responsible for Katherine Grey's fate. But do I have a choice? Sir Francis is unwavering. He won't take pity on me.

"It would be a strange coincidence if they met by chance."

"Do you suspect Lady Katherine Grey is in league with the Spanish?"

"Why is this beginning to feel like an interrogation?"

"Answer the question, my lady. You are in no danger. In the game of politics, a scrap of information can make all the difference. You've been living in close quarters with to her and would know her better than any spy who simply watched from afar."

"Then no, I don't believe so." I clear my throat, feeling the anxiety ease. "She isn't ambitious and is more concerned about the banal things, like the colour of a ribbon that might suit her, rather than plotting. If anything, it is the ambassador who should be watched. Lady Katherine might not even know what is going on."

"You believe she is a figurehead, then?"

"Yes." I say, hoping this will be enough for him.

In the days that follow, guilt racks me over the matter. I've done my duty and upheld my oath to serve the queen before all others. But what if she is innocent? Surely, I cannot be the only one who reported what they saw, and Walsingham has countless spies everywhere. He wouldn't act without corroborating my report.

One thing is certain—the queen has been told something. She is not shy about showing her displeasure with Katherine and constantly snubs her. The following day, the queen was listening to Katherine play the virginals when she interrupts her.

"Why is it that those with the least skill feel compelled to play the longest?" she asks Blanche Parry rather loudly. The older woman scolds her former ward, but others who heard giggle.

Katherine goes white, but to her credit finishes the

song before rising from her seat and bowing to the queen. "Apologies if my playing has offended you."

The queen didn't bother looking at her. Instead, she looks at Lady Mary Sidney. "Mary, why don't you play for us?"

She rushes forward, happy to have been singled out.

Katherine is left standing awkwardly in the middle of all of this. As she retreats to the back of the room, our eyes meet. The hairs on the back of my neck stand on end as she directs all that hot anger towards me. I know she blames me for the queen's rudeness. And here I thought I could rise above all the petty squabbles and gossip at court.

"No, Lady Dorothy, on the seventh count you turn left not right," the dance master watching me corrects me once again.

I come to a stop, my cheeks flush from the heat and embarrassment. Pulling out a kerchief, I dab at my fore-head. We've been at this for hours, and I'm no closer to memorising the steps for the masque.

"Again." The dance master takes a seat and nods to the musicians to strike up the song again.

"Perhaps it is best to leave it for the day," I say. "My two left feet will fall off at this rate, and I'll be of even less use to the queen."

I can tell he's not used to hearing arguments from his

students, and he shakes his head. "Again and again until you can dance with the grace of a swan."

I hear a snort of laughter from the far end of the room. Katherine Grey is sitting on a chair watching me, content as a cat. Her friend Jane and younger sister Mary sit beside her. She leans to one side as if to whisper to them, but she speaks loudly enough for me to hear.

"There's only so far you can train a monkey. Breeding always shows." Her eyes flick to mine and her lips twist into a malicious grin. "I'd be too embarrassed to show my face at court if I couldn't even learn a dance."

My back stiffens, but I focus my attention on the dance master, tapping out the time. I will master this.

I take three more tries to get it right. I'm allowed to stop but told to return the following morning once my duties are over to practise some more.

"You are not a natural dancer who feels the music." He sniffs as if this is a travesty. "But that doesn't mean you cannot learn. Practice. That's all it takes."

"I will apply myself," I swear. The last thing I want is to make a fool of myself in front of Katherine Grey. It's childish to think I am competing with someone younger than myself, but I will never gain authority over her if I don't best her in every way.

That night, dressed in only a linen shift, I prance around my room going over the steps until my legs quiver from exhaustion. If anything, I'm persistent. It's no longer about proving Katherine wrong. If I'm going to survive at court, I cannot afford to embarrass myself in front of the queen by failing to be a proper gentlewoman.

The masque goes off without a hitch. Prince Erik of Sweden's envoy is welcomed with great fanfare. The queen is dressed in a gown of blue gauze and silk to complement the colours of his house. He waxes poetic about how awestruck he is over her beauty until I see her attention begin to wane.

Queen Elizabeth gestures for him to sit beside her, and the musicians take that as their cue to start the music. The master of ceremonies steps forward bowing and says a few words in Swedish. The envoy has learned French and Latin, and some say he's studying English as well, but the gesture of goodwill is greatly appreciated.

"We have prepared elaborate entertainments for you," the queen says to the envoy, who nods excitedly. He glances around the grand hall, laden with beautiful tapestries and ornate linens. He can see the wealth of England on display.

I retreat with the other ladies-in-waiting who aren't too old to take part, and we don our costumes for the masque.

We are fairies dancing in a forested glade when handsome knights come across us and start to woo us with song, poetry, and a dance.

With chagrin, I note my partner is Sir William Pickering. His hands are hot on my hips as he lifts me up into the air. Taken by the moment, I allow him to draw me closer before twirling away. I cannot get lost in the moment as keeping in time with the music is paramount.

To his credit, when I step on his toes, he doesn't make a sound.

The dance ends, and we bow low to the queen and then to the prince's envoy, who stands and applauds our performance.

"Well done. Bravo," he calls out. He's about to sit down when the queen rises to her feet. A maid rushes forward and unpins the long formal train of her gown.

Catching on to what she wants, the envoy bows low to her and offers her his outstretched hand.

She accepts, and he leads her on to the dance floor.

We move aside for them, and the musicians strike up a song.

In the alcove out of the way, Sir William stays by my side. Out of sight, his hand trails down my spine, tantalisingly slow. As I gaze up at him, it is clear what is on his mind. In a different life, perhaps, I would be tempted by the beguiling smile and handsome features.

Though I grin at him, I inch away from him. "Pardon me, sir."

"My fairy escapes me already?" he whispers.

"Of course. Have you read nothing of the ancient Greek texts? Mythical creatures can never be tamed or captured for long. It always ends in tragedy."

"Then I am glad that you are a mortal woman."

"Perhaps," I tease. "But you will find my sense of duty trumps all other desires."

"Would you be opposed to me attempting to distract you away from your duty?"

I glance into his eyes. "No, I suppose I would not. Though it might be better for you if you try elsewhere."

"Being in your presence alone is enough for me. As long as you don't send me from your side, I am content."

I arch a brow. Those were passionate words. But this is the court. I would be a fool if I took them at face value. However, knowing this doesn't stop the thrill that runs through me.

The arrival of the Swedish envoy changes the queen's policy towards the Grey sisters. Rather than trying to keep them hidden in obscurity, she promotes them. They go from being merely maids in waiting to being part of the queen's privy chamber and thus, are close to her day and night. She is kinder to them as well. Their mother is truly ill and shows no signs of improving. I watch all this filled with an anxiety that I cannot place. Katherine, rather than being more careful, chooses to flaunt her newfound power, which is alienating her from her friends.

"Look!" Katherine giggles as she struts around the room, half-dressed to show us a new bodice gifted to her by the queen herself.

She escapes her exasperated maids, who bend to pick up the gold pins that fall on to the carpet.

I motion for Mary to ensure no pins are missed. The last thing we need is the queen pricking her foot on one.

A few of the other ladies come forward to admire the

beautiful work on the bodice and the frontlet that goes with it.

"It's French, but the lace is Italian," Katherine says, pushing out her chest, her fingers grazing the delicate work.

"Flemish," I whisper under my breath. Catherine Knollys smiles at my cheek. We are folding away the queen's linen and stockings for the day, ensuring everything is accounted for.

Katherine Grey returns to the front of the looking glass. Her head has been swollen with pride over her youthful beauty. It is common knowledge that many lords and foreign princes have applied for her hand in marriage. No doubt she's starting to see herself as a princess in line for the English throne. To her credit, it may be true. The queen has not come close to accepting a proposal of marriage and forestalls, even the discussion of the topic. The longer she hesitates, the more important the Grey sisters become.

"I can't believe the Spanish want her." I glance at Katherine with scorn. News leaked out that the Spanish ambassador has been arrested. He was plotting to whisk her out of the kingdom and marry her to King Philip's son and heir. Undoubtedly, they would use Katherine Grey as an excuse to invade England. "She might be foolish, but I couldn't imagine her agreeing to such a dangerous plan."

"Exactly." Catherine Knollys pulls the stockings I have bunched in my hands and carefully smooths them out. "She is foolish and thus, it would be easy to lead her astray. She'd be biddable to whatever plan they put before her if they were to tempt her vanity. That is why the queen is eager to make her a friend rather than an enemy."

"I'm simply surprised the Spanish haven't thought of another way..."

"She's Catholic," Catherine Knollys says, with some derision. "That's all they really care about. She's of marriageable age, and she's not in the hands of the French."

I know she's referring to Mary Queen of Scots, married to the French Dauphin and future French king. If they have issue, that child will inherit both Scotland and France. It was a brilliant political match but has caused England no end of trouble. The queen has sent her ambassadors to France to work out a treaty with the French King to ensure that Mary relinquishes her right to the English throne. Every letter that returns from Cecil is met with anger. The French King has taken to calling Mary, Queen of Scotland and England. He even had the audacity to have a new coat of arms drawn up for her. The queen flew into a rage when she heard.

Out of the corner of my eye I catch Katherine tugging her bodice lower, exposing far more skin than is decent.

"I don't believe her majesty intended for you to expose yourself when she gifted that to you," I say, unable to hold my tongue.

Kat Ashley glances her way. "Goodness me. Pull up this instant." As one of the queen's principal ladies,

Kat Ashley rules the roost, and Katherine Grey's maids rush to adjust the bodice back into its proper place.

Katherine rolls her eyes but has the decency to let them do their work. "It's the new fashion. You wouldn't understand." Her eyes travel over my dress with obvious pity.

My hand touches the neckerchief I wear underneath my gown. It's a white gauzy silk, a present from my aunt on the day I wed William. I still treasure it and wear it often. The fashions might change, yet married women and widows cannot go around uncovered, regardless of my inclination.

Katherine Grey seems to think this is some sort of victory over me, but no matter how irritated I might feel, I will not let myself be drawn into some foolish argument.

In the summer, as the heat leaves the city sweltering and full of illness, the queen prepares to move to one of her summer palaces away from London. I ask for leave to go visit my children and am given leave—reluctantly—to go for three weeks.

"You are lucky," Catherine says as she helps me pack away my things into trunks.

"The queen won't allow you to leave?"

She shakes her head. "Not that I would wish to leave her majesty's service, but it's hard to be apart from my family for so long."

I reach over and give her hand a tight squeeze. "Your

eldest children are of an age to come to court, at least. We shall have to think of places for them."

She smiles and gives a nod.

I leave Windsor with two manservants and a maid for escort.

A letter tucked into my pocket has me changing my plans. My aunt is unwell and wishes to see me.

The day I set out, the ground is soggy, and I arrive at my aunt's residence with my skirts caked in an inch of mud.

Her lady-in-waiting takes me up to her solar. My aunt is stretched out onto the daybed wrapped in blankets, looking greatly diminished.

"Your grace," I say with a deep curtsey when her head turns towards me.

She inclines her head. I cannot make out from her expression if she is unhappy to see me or not.

"How are you?" I approach, taking a seat by her.

"Poorly. You should have your eyes checked, dear girl, if you cannot tell. Perhaps, you have gone blind." She stretches out a hand towards me. I clasp her cold frail hands in mine and place a kiss on the back of her palm before kissing both cheeks.

Her eyes follow my every move.

"You've developed some very smart manners since you've been at court. You are far more graceful in your movements and careful in how you pay your respects."

"It's all a credit to you. Had I not improved at all, I would have been a very poor student. Not that I was ever some creature plucked from the jungle," I say, looking away from her.

When I glance back at her, she is grinning, the gaps in her teeth more prominent. "That's exactly what you were when I plucked you from your parents' house all those years ago. I daresay court has suited you. You're far more confident now and carry yourself with an air of gravitas."

"I don't know about that, aunt," I say, rearranging my skirts just to distract me from the embarrassment.

"Did you come to see what I've left you in my will?" she asks.

"Not at all. Don't you dare speak like that. Your doctors assured me you just need rest." I hush her, then I draw out a small pouch from my pocket and put it on her lap. "I was concerned when I received your letter, but I also came with the specific purpose of returning this to you."

Her brow arches as she turns the pouch over into her outstretched hand. The amethyst pansy brooch falls into her palm, which wobbles with the effort.

"If you were smarter, you would've kept this for yourself or sold it for a tidy profit, and if I were to ever ask you about it, you could claim you lost it."

"You know I would never do that, aunt."

She clicks her tongue on the roof of her mouth. "It's imperative that you put aside some of your convictions."

"Aunt, if I lost this one, you wouldn't be so quick to lend me any more jewels. You see, I'm far more calculating than you think."

This has her laughing but before long it turns into a wheezing cough that sends spasms wracking her whole body. I grip her hand as if that might stop her.

When the fit is over, a maid offers her a cup of hot spiced ale. I take it from her and urge my aunt to drink as much as she can.

"I need to rest. Don't worry about me," she says, seeing how concerned I look.

I read to her until she falls asleep and then go to speak to her physicians.

"We fear it is her lungs. She caught a chill in the spring, and after that, she never fully recovered. Our tinctures can only do so much, and she is a woman of advanced years." They can't bring themselves to say they believe my aunt is dying, and really, they cannot know. The great duchess has survived far worse—a miracle could happen.

Yet, given that I don't know when I can leave court again, this may be the last time I see my aunt. Without hesitation, I change my plans and send a note to my mother to let her know I am delayed.

If my aunt is displeased by the attention I lavish on her the next day, she says nothing. When I do at last take my leave of her, a lump of anxiety has formed in my throat. I manage to hold back the tears until I'm well out of sight, and then a fresh wave of guilt overtakes me as I feel as though I'm already mourning her. Fearful of inviting bad luck, I wipe my eyes and force myself to smile.

Once I am surrounded by my children, the pain

eases. They are as delighted to see me as I am them. We spend the following days in a whirlwind of activity. We ride, play games, and read together. I teach my daughters the dances I've learned at the court and tell my sons of the tournaments I've witnessed. They are enthralled by my stories and eager for more.

My marriage took place during a tumultuous time in England. My children had been an added stress. I loved them the best I could and tried to provide them with the finest life could offer, but it's not until now that I realise how distracted I've been. Back then there was no time to arrange picnics—we were too concerned about where our next meal would come from. Fleeing England compounded those matters.

Did I make a mistake going to Court? Would I have been happier here with my children? The question nags me and nearly taints my happiness. I push it aside to focus on them. Time passes too quickly as it is and before long, I find I'm back on the road. I join the court at Ipswich with a heavy heart. If things could've been another way, I would've stayed but duty comes first.

CHAPTER 7

I slip back into court life as if I never left. My days are spent fetching gloves, embroidering, and accompanying the queen. Yet, I am taken aback by the tense atmosphere. The queen has still not decided one way or another which of her many suitors she will choose to marry. Bets are laid and fortunes lost as the days pass without a word.

For every step forward, she takes two back.

It all comes to a head when the court travels to Nonsuch Palace, currently the home of the Earl of Arundel, and a fight breaks out.

"You mean to insult me," Robert Dudley accuses the earl.

Twenty years his junior, he has no shame as he continues to berate the earl, who is quickly turning red in the face.

"How so?" Arundel demands, all but sputtering.

It's impossible for me to avert my gaze from the

disaster playing out before me. The queen is below in the garden, walking with the Spanish ambassador, while we are in the gallery preparing for a banquet in her honour. Servants and noblemen alike are coming and going.

"You put me in rooms unbefitting to my station," Robert says, his voice loud and clear for all to hear. There is no doubt in my mind that this is a calculated move on his part.

The earl, who has always been an impatient man, puffs up, indignant at the accusations made against him.

"And what station is that?" he sneers. "You were allotted rooms as befits your rank and birth."

Robert Dudley remains calm. "On the merit of being the queen's Master of the Horse alone, I should be given rooms closer to her majesty's. Without me, this visit couldn't have taken place."

I'm so distracted that I nearly drop the vase of fresh-cut flowers I'm arranging for her majesty's table when Sir William Pickering bends to whisper in my ear. "The ragged staff is poking the bear."

His jest earns him a grin, but I swat him away just the same.

"I thought the Dudley crest also had a bear on it. Besides, the bear isn't one of the heraldic symbols the earl uses anymore."

"Having gone head-to-head with Arundel in the past, I can assure you the man is an angry bear. Especially when cornered."

"And just as powerful?" I question, my eyes flicking

over to the two men who look as though they might come to blows.

"Dudley is not without his friends, but I doubt even he can move the earl."

"Shall we bet on it?" I have caught the movement in the garden below. The queen is returning.

"A shilling."

"Done," I say, my eyes dancing with mischief.

"Why do I get the sense that I have already lost?" he says, teasing.

"I am done arguing with mere words," the Earl of Arundel's voice booms in the gallery. "Shall we draw swords?"

Before Robert can respond, the queen arrives flocked by both the Spanish ambassador and the Swedish envoy with four of her closest ladies-in-waiting following closely behind.

"I thought you invited me here to be entertained, yet I arrive to find you have a very different sort of activity in mind." Queen Elizabeth fixes both men with an icy glare.

They fall to their knees, prostrating themselves before her.

"Apologies, Your Grace." The earl speaks first. "I meant no harm."

"I certainly hope so. You know how I feel about duelling."

Pickering snorts behind me, but covers it up with a cough. Not too long ago, Arundel challenged him to a duel. He refused to accept, something that offended the earl more. I can see why William wouldn't wish to fight him. Despite his bravado, anyone can tell he's not a healthy man. His age alone should disqualify him from any armed combat. Everyone can see this, except for the man himself.

"Both of you rise and explain yourselves," Queen Elizabeth commands.

Robert remains where he is. The queen approaches. The silence in the gallery is stifling. We can all hear the swish of her gown as she approaches him.

Her hand touches the top of his head. "Did I not command you to rise?"

He says something I can't quite hear, but a wide smile spreads across her features. The queen turns to look at the foreign dignitaries she has been entertaining and winks at them. Then she turns to the earl. "There's been a mistake with his rooms. You will see that the mistake is amended, will you not, my dearest Arundel?"

The earl flushes scarlet and bows. "Of course, Your Grace."

I lean towards William and say, "I will expect payment without delay."

"Fear not, you shall have it."

The way he mutters those words has my breath hitching. When I gaze up at him, I'm lost in the moment, taken by his handsome features and the intensity of his eyes.

Distinctly aware of where we are, I step away from him.

The queen returns to the ambassador and with a sigh, loudly declares, "If only there was one with the strength to wrangle these wild courtiers of mine."

The earl stepped forward. "Just say the word, Your Grace."

Behind him, Robert Dudley flares with indignation. Catching this, Elizabeth smiles sweetly at the earl and offers him her hand.

As the feast begins, he's the one who leads her to her seat.

Rumours begin to circulate that the earl has secretly proposed to her and she's accepted him. Heavy bets are laid for the duration of the visit. Whether the queen has caught wind of them doesn't seem to matter. She pays the earl every respect and attention.

Only as she changes out of her formal gowns and sits at her desk reading over her correspondence does it become clear to me that her mind is far from marriage—any marriage.

She catches me watching her and motions me to come closer.

"Did you see the Spanish ambassador today? How did he look?"

"Despondent," I say.

She chuckles, setting aside her letter and picking up another.

"I hope you will do well off this."

"Your majesty?"

"The betting. I hope you've thrown your hat into the ring. You could win a fortune. Don't miss the opportunity."

"I wouldn't dare presume to know Your Majesty's mind."

She looks amused. "Unlike so many of my other courtiers." She stares at the letter in her hand. I cannot see what is written, but I recognise the emperor's seal. "Men give up so easily when they think they are losing. It's disappointing to see," she says.

I'm prompted to speak candidly to her and say, "There is one I doubt would ever give up."

Her brow arches, and she waits for me to finish. My cheeks grow hot. I had been thinking of William Pickering's persistence, but I know the answer she is expecting.

"Lord Robert Dudley, Your Majesty."

She laughs. "Yes. He's the—" She catches herself. "See if you can find Throckmorton. We must settle the matter over the cost of the renovations of my apartments at Whitehall."

I curtsey and rush to do as she bids.

The next day, the Spanish ambassador's sulky demeanour adds credence to the rumour mill that something is going on between the queen and Arundel. I remain silent on the subject even though I am offered several bribes for information.

Then on the day of our departure, the queen addresses the earl.

"I've enjoyed my visit to Nonsuch so much, I loathe the thought of leaving."

He inclines his head. "You are more than welcome to prolong your stay."

"I wish I could," she sighs. Then her lips curl into a grin. I'm prepared for mischief, but even I am surprised by what she says next. "But before long, Lord Henry, I shall return and make this a happy home."

Even Lord Robert Dudley, waiting at her side, stiffens in surprise. His eyes flick to her as if he were eager to pull her aside and ask her to explain herself. He might have won himself rooms closer to her during their stay here, but ultimately, I can see he fears what will become of him once she marries.

The Earl of Arundel is pleased and chooses this moment to present the queen with an extravagant gift he has prepared.

"Please accept this gift so you may remember me and your time here fondly," he says, placing a kiss on her hand.

It's hard to maintain a straight face when I notice how crestfallen the foreign dignitaries have become at this display. Months of meetings and planning might come to nothing. Others in the crowd have brightened. I imagine they are counting their winnings. They are bound to be disappointed.

The queen waves farewell to the earl's assembled household, then turns to mount her waiting horse. For a moment, our eyes meet, and we share a knowing smile.

Now that the summer progress has ended, the queen returns to Hampton Court. Our day-to-day routine should be returning to some semblance of predictability, yet in many regards, it has not.

Lord Robert Dudley, always a favourite, has managed to entrench himself deeper in the queen's affections. Wherever she goes, he goes. Day and night, he's allowed access to the queen.

It's hard for anyone to approach her without first going through him.

"A king in all but name," Lady Catherine Knollys whispers to me one evening after returning from her husband's rooms.

"He's a married man. She refuses to consider Englishmen like the Earl of Arundel or even Sir William Pickering, who both come from established wealthy English families. Assuming he was free to marry, could you truly see her stooping so low to accept him?" I ask, freeing my hair from the tight braids. My neck aches, and I roll my shoulders back.

"You've seen how Dudley fawns over her. He has a way of managing her." Catherine whispers this last part. "Today when she asked for her lute, he captured her hand and pulled the glove off her hand, one finger at a time, then tucked it into his pocket. The Duke of Norfolk was present and could barely contain his rage." She sighs, sitting down on the edge of the bed. "My husband says vile rumours about the pair of them are all over the city. The commoners don't believe she's a virgin queen any longer."

I would laugh at the ridiculousness of the rumour, but it is a dangerous one. "When would it have even been possible for her to run off with a lover? The queen is never alone. What vile person would spread such lies?"

She shrugs. "Does it matter? The point is people believe it. Watching them together, is it so farfetched to think that she would allow him other liberties in private?"

I glance away. I've seen how destructive rumours can be. Did they not destroy my own family?

"Cecil is beside himself. He approached my husband for his support for the marriage with the Archduke Charles if the one with the Scottish heir falls through."

"Is the Earl of Aaran coming to England? I thought he was in hiding?"

She checks the door to make sure we aren't being watched and nods. "But even if he does, the queen may not find him agreeable. I think given the recent threats from the French, Cecil would prefer the queen marry the archduke."

"She's rejected him once already," I point out.

"Neither of them is married yet. Until that day, there will always be a chance they can agree on the terms of marriage treaty."

"Or France could continue making incursions and force the queen's hand."

"Or that," Catherine says, with exasperation. "I'm so tired of feeling as though we are threatened from all quarters. This is our home. I don't want to be forced to flee or see my family torn apart by war."

"We must pray and trust our queen to protect us."

She looks as if she would say more, but she bites her tongue. I understand how helpless she is feeling. I am in the same position as her.

The next day, as I mount my horse, I find a small sealed note pinned to my saddle. I open it quickly before anyone can see.

Inside is a poem written in an unfamiliar scrawl.

Tresses of sable entwine about my heart.
Never has one captured me so.

Careful to keep my expression blank, I slip the note into the sleeve of my gown. My head turns and I examine the assembled courtiers. It's then I notice William watching me. His expression is warm as he touches his cap and tilts his head in acknowledgement.

I'm flattered but my heart doesn't pound in my chest, for I know a hard truth: his intentions cannot be honourable. This is a man who sought to woo a queen. I am a woman without a dowry and a large brood of children that would have to be provided for. He might flirt with me, send me secret little notes, but it means nothing. If I pursued a secret affair with him, I'd ruin my chances at court.

No. I must protect myself.

I make sure to keep my distance and we never speak for the duration of the ride.

At night after the queen has gone to bed, I feed the poem into the fire. I don't say a word to anyone. In the future, I should take more care not to invite the flirtatious attentions of the gentlemen of the court. Still, I find myself wondering if I'm jumping to conclusions. Later, when Catherine asks why I look so melancholic, I try to wave away her concerns.

"There's a deep sadness in your eyes," she says, squeezing my hand.

"I was thinking of my husband, and I feel guilty," I say, knowing it's true. "I was wondering what it would've been like if we'd been passionately in love. He was never one to bring me gifts or write me poems. We might scoff at Dudley and his antics but—"

"They are romantic," she interrupts with a sigh. "Yes, it's true. You never know what the future will bring. Perhaps you will find yourself a handsome suitor at court." She winks.

I laugh. "I fear I will grow old and weary waiting for him to arrive."

"I daresay with that attitude you will."

CHAPTER 8

"What do you mean he's at your house?" the queen snaps.

We've managed to capture the queen's hair into a gold cord net. I attempting to pin it into place with pearl pins, but the task is proving impossible for even a seasoned veteran like Mary Sidney.

"Your grace," Cecil says, taking a step back. "An alliance between the two of you would be advantageous to you both."

It's a gentle reminder, but I can tell from his exasperated face he's reaching the limit of his patience. A few weeks ago, he was given permission to arrange this very meeting with the express command to keep it secret.

Predictably, Queen Elizabeth seethes. "I expect you have a priest waiting in the wings as well."

He bows his head. "Of course not. Unless you command it. You know I am your loyal servant and would never act against your express wishes and that of

England. There is no expectation on his side other than to have the honour of meeting you in person."

Lady Mary Sidney touches her shoulder. "Your majesty, please sit still so I can finish with your hair."

"Oh, leave it alone," she says, pulling the net off her head and letting her red-gold tresses tumble free down her back. "How irritating to always be poked and prodded."

Mary glances my way, and we share a strained smile as all our hard work comes undone.

Without a word, I pick up the discarded net while Mary collects the pearl pins.

Taking his chances now that the storm has passed Cecil tries again. "You are scheduled to dine at my London house this evening. Perhaps it would be the perfect opportunity to be introduced in secret."

Elizabeth rubs at her temple.

"Shall I have the physician prepare something for your headache?" I ask.

"A brisk walk is all the cure I need. Where is Lord Robert?"

As his sister, I leave it to Mary Sidney to answer this awkward question. What will the queen say if she knows he has slipped out this morning to visit his wife in Lincolnshire? Surely, he asked the queen's permission, but given her current mood...

"He will be back tomorrow," Mary says, keeping her tone light.

The queen's lips purse in displeasure, but she doesn't comment. Turning back to Cecil, she smiles at him at last. "Very well, I shall meet this suitor of mine tonight."

~

I am among those honoured to attend the queen during her visit. Cecil has spared no expense when it comes to entertaining her. The hall is decked in garlands of flowers, an endless stream of musicians play soft lilting music, mummers perform and then there is even a play. Only later into the evening, after the queen has danced and feasted to her heart's content, does Cecil pull her away.

Mary Sidney and I accompany her. My own heart is pounding in my chest as we weave our way around the corridors to a private office at the back of the house.

Cecil himself opens the door, and we step inside the brightly lit room to find the Earl of Aaran staring out the window.

It appears he did not hear us come in, as he doesn't turn. We can see his lips are moving though we can hear no sound. The queen's eyebrow arches, and Cecil clears his throat.

This draws the earl's attention. He spins on his heel, and we finally got a good look at him. He is well-built. Shorter than her majesty, but with even features that the queen might find handsome. His chestnut-brown hair and round plaintive eyes gave him a kind aspect. This would not be a man who would dominate his wife.

He bows low when he sees the queen.

"I've long thought of this moment, Your Grace," he

says. "Thank you for honouring me and for the help you gave me in evading my captors. I feared for my life."

She bows her head and offers him her hand.

He places a kiss on it but just as quickly moves away. A long silence follows. Cecil's shoulders visibly slump. He knows how particular our mistress is. She's also surrounded by hundreds of charismatic men who play court to her night and day. As much as she might claim to only have the interests of England in mind when making her marriage, we know she won't be able to commit herself to a man who cannot make conversation.

"What were you doing when we walked in?" the queen asks.

The Earl of Arran is taken aback by such a question. "I was looking out the window. The garden below is beautiful."

"Even in winter?"

"Certainly. I use my imagination to fill in the blanks," he says, offering a weak smile.

There's something odd about his turn of phrase but I can't quite put my finger on it. Silence falls upon the room. Cecil is at his wits' end. The look he gives the earl is imploring, yet the earl either doesn't notice or is content to ignore it.

"And how are you liking England thus far?" the queen asks. She hasn't bothered to take a seat, and from that alone I know this interview will be over fast. How many months of careful planning went into this? Cecil is trying to hide his irritation, but he's no doubt already finding some way to turn this to his advantage.

"It's very nice. Thank you once again for rescuing me." The earl's eyes dart between Cecil and Elizabeth. "I am most grateful to be here. I hope to see more of your court one day. If I can ever be of service to you, please let me know."

"Of course," the queen responds, her tone reserved. "Is that all?"

"I wouldn't seek to presume..." The earl pauses, then, clearing his throat, says, "I had hoped you might consider me a worthy husband. As the heir to the Scottish throne, we might unite our two nations."

"We shall see," the queen says blandly. "It's late. I bid you a good night."

Without waiting for either of us, she is out the door.

Cecil hangs back to whisper a few words to the earl, who merely nods and seems content to return to staring out the window.

As we follow the queen, I ask Mary Sidney, "Is there something wrong with the earl?"

She gives me an incredulous shrug. "I think Prince Erik has more of a chance of marrying the queen than he does. Despite him being richer and handsome."

Cecil pushes past us and catches up to the queen. We hang back, watching her berate him.

"I could never marry a man like that," she hisses at him. "Can't string two words together."

"Your grace, the honour of being in your presence overtook him. A marriage between the two of you—"

"Would be out of the question," she says, cutting him off.

Cecil hangs his head low. "Yes, Your Majesty. Then we must consider the archduke again."

She lets out a frustrated sigh. "Another day, spirit. I feel as though I'm a doe hunted by my suitors. No matter which way I turn, one is there, lying in wait."

"Then Your Majesty should pick one. That is the only way this issue will go away."

She gives a high-pitched laugh. "Hardly. That would simply introduce other problems."

"The succession is a pressing issue that keeps all your councillors awake at night. The health and future of the nation is at stake."

"My nation." Her eyes flash dangerously. "And I understand better than anyone the heavy burden the crown brings with it. God has chosen me to safeguard the realm. I am the one who has to select the safest course to take, and I shall not be swayed by you or anyone else."

He takes a step back as though she has struck him and bows his head. "I never meant to presume, Your Grace."

The queen returns to the great hall.

Moments later, we are being escorted by all the visitors back to the royal barge. The queen sits wrapped in furs against the damp night air, with Mary and I on either side of her.

"There was something peculiar about that man," Queen Elizabeth says.

"He certainly wouldn't be a charming addition to your court," Lady Mary says. Of course, she is trying to protect her brother's position as the queen's favourite.

"There are many others who would serve much better as consort."

"On the other hand, you would never have to worry about him overshadowing you," I say. She turns to me, eyes crinkled with amusement. "Though you might have trouble with him putting you to sleep with his boring conversation. Hardly productive for the health of the nation or the making of heirs."

She laughs. "I'd rebuke you for being so forward with me if it wasn't true."

"The very least he could've done was pay you a proper compliment," Mary says.

"I suspect he might be mad," I add. "He seemed more intrigued by the dried-up hedges outside than by being in the presence of the Queen of England."

"Peculiar, wasn't it?" the queen says, now back in good humour.

But remembering what Cecil said a few days ago, I hesitantly bring up the continued threat of France. "However unlikely a candidate he is, there is a reason Cecil was so insistent on you meeting him. The French are still moving against you and have yet to sign the treaty acknowledging you as queen. If they were to suspect you working with the Protestant Scots lords, they might hurry to rectify the treaty to protect their own interests in Scotland."

She looks impressed as studies me closer. "You are more entrenched in politics than I realised, Lady Dorothy."

I bow my head to hide a smile, not wishing to appear proud. "I only wish to serve you."

"Well, regardless of my decision and how unsuitable he is as a suitor, we can keep the French guessing a bit longer."

The following day, despite the disastrous meeting, rumours begin to circulate that the queen has met with the Scottish heir and found him pleasing. Everyone watches the queen, and she, rather than contradicting rumours, goes around court with a secret smile on her face and wears tartan.

Exasperated by her behaviour, Cecil doesn't know what to make of it and is forced to play along when she tells him she wishes for a private audience with the Scottish envoy.

The French are quick to act. The French ambassador brings her a personally penned letter from the King of France himself along with a diamond brooch the queen admires. He then begs her to reconsider marriage to the earl and speaks ill of him, suggesting that the queen shouldn't lower herself to marry someone of such dubious birth.

"I cannot allow you to speak thus of Lord James. He is dear to us." The queen places her hand over her heart.

"Apologies, Your Majesty. I had believed that you were looking for a match among your English gentlemen and not a foreign one. My king would be happy to suggest a French match for you. It would be someone far more suitable and may bring our nations closer together."

The queen, outraged, sends him away and refuses to see him again for a week as punishment.

Robert Dudley, back from the country, is surprised to arrive home to find the court in such disarray.

The queen doesn't show him any sign of displeasure at his absence, but neither does she assure him she isn't intending to marry the Earl of Aaran. Watching how nervous Robert is, I doubt he'll be willing to risk leaving court again.

Dudley is quick to add his voice behind those who believe the earl would be an unsuitable match. Two factions form at court while the queen goes on pretending to consider the match and even plans her upcoming nuptials. I wonder what her bridegroom thinks about all this, or if he even knows.

We are playing bowls on the green when I find I can no longer avoid William Pickering.

"It feels like an age since I was last in your company," he says.

I merely nod.

"And what do you think about all this business with the earl?" William Pickering asks, changing the topic. "Do you believe she is serious about marrying him?"

"I couldn't say." I roll my ball and miss the mark.

"Not even if I were to slip a few coins into your pockets?"

I glare at him.

"It was a jest. Have I done something to upset you?"

"Not at all," I say. Really, I've been meaning to make it clear to him I'm not interested in any romantic liaison.

He leans closer to whisper. "You've been avoiding me ever since I wrote you that poem. Was it so terribly written?"

"I was very flattered, but I cannot imagine why you'd write to me at all."

He grins. "I thought we were becoming fast friends."

"Our ideas of friendship might be very different."

He frowns at that and runs a hand over his smooth-shaven face.

"Perhaps I've been cold, and I'm sorry for that. As for the queen, I am not lying. I truly never know what she intends to do. From one moment to another, she changes her mind."

"You may be the most honest lady attending her right now. Many are selling information, and as you can guess, all the accounts vary."

I chuckle. "You must've meant I'm the most foolish for not taking advantage of my position as I ought to."

"Quite the contrary. You are a breath of fresh air, and I don't plan on letting you out of my sights any time soon."

My face must be blushing a brilliant shade of red because he smiles, his gloved hand touching my cheek. I should pull away. But I don't.

Dudley has arranged a pageant on the river, but the weather has turned colder. I volunteer to go fetch the queen's furred mantle. Taking a shortcut, I run through the inner courtyard with its hedges and statues, when I hear a sound.

I stop short and listen.

"Someone's out there," a female voice giggles.

"Shh, I'll go see. We are safe," a familiar voice says.

I swallow hard. It's William Pickering. While there was no understanding between us, it still stings to come across him meeting in secret with who I can only assume is another lover. Fearing discovery, I wait for them to be distracted so I can leave without having an awkward encounter. The tell-tale rustle of fabric fills the air. I start towards the exit, but my feet kick up some stones.

Out of the darkness, he emerges. When he catches sight of me, his eyes go wide and his lips part ready with some explanation.

In a very unladylike fashion, I lift my skirt and flee as fast as I can into the corridor beyond. I hear him calling after me, but I don't stop.

In my haste, I don't pay attention to where I'm going, and I collide with something solid. A man catches hold of me by my arms and keeps me from falling to the ground.

Rather than being thankful, I snap, "Unhand me," before yanking myself out of his loose grip. There's a flash of amusement in his eye that checks me. Having just fled one man, I am simply unprepared to find myself in the arms of another.

"Pardon me, my lady," he says with a bow. He's

wearing the queen's livery, yet I can't quite place him. Is he a secretary? An usher?

"I am the one who should apologise. Thank you for your assistance." I try to arrange my skirts.

"Allow me to introduce myself. I am Sir Thomas Blount, cousin and personal secretary to Lord Robert Dudley. Is there anything else I can help you with?" He glances behind me to see what I'd been fleeing from.

"Ah. No. Thank you." I stop to catch my breath. Inwardly, I scold myself for sounding like a fool. "I'm on an errand for the queen."

"Are you in any danger?"

"No," I say too quickly, only to feel compelled to look over my shoulder. Pickering is nowhere to be seen. I visibly relax.

His brow raises. "Why don't I believe you?"

I frown. Why is it any of his business? I eye him. Clearly, the man has a chivalrous streak in him and won't let the matter rest. In any other situation, I would've found him sweet and been grateful to him.

Relenting, I say, "Because it's only half-true. I am on an errand for her majesty. I just happened across a private moment between two people, and out of embarrassment I ran away. Now you will call me a coward, but that's the truth of it. Am I free to go?"

His smile widens. "I wouldn't call you a coward. I can only imagine how embarrassed and awkward it was for a lady of your reputation to come across two lovers."

"I never said they were lovers."

"You didn't have to. Your blush gave you away."

Squaring back my shoulders, I face him straight on. "I'm not some delicate maiden. I'm a widow and a mother to six children."

"That's something one forgets about you, Lady Dorothy."

I'm taken aback. "You know who I am?"

"Of course. You are hard to miss."

He doesn't smile coyly or take the opportunity to shuffle closer. Instead, he merely looks at me as if he told me the sky is blue. It's this sincerity that makes my heart beat faster. But sincere or not, listening to flattery almost got me into trouble. So I dig my fingernails into my palms and resolve to ignore him and his kind compliments.

"Well, now at least we are on equal footing," I say, stepping around him. The temptation to hurry away is there, but I check myself. With all proper politeness, I curtsey. "Good evening, Sir Thomas."

CHAPTER 9

By the end of September, the game is up. For all her teasing and pretending, it has become clear to everyone that the Earl of Arran will not be the queen's husband. He is now in Scotland and working with the Protestant lords there.

When the Scottish envoy suggests a match between the earl and Katherine Grey, the queen appears amenable.

As for Katherine herself, I am surprised to see how panicked she is at the prospect of an international marriage.

Lady Jane Seymour is always by her side, holding her hand to steady her. It is a peculiar scene, but no one else comments on it. Perhaps she had hopes for a grander Spanish alliance. Whatever is going on with her, there is no time to dwell on it as the queen has once again flung herself on the marriage market.

Thinking the queen was only holding out to negotiate

better terms, the archduke's envoy once again proposes Charles as the perfect husband for her. With rumours of growing French ambitions, the queen needs more allies and doesn't reject the idea. Cecil is instructed to honour him with a private dinner, and the following day the queen plans to grant the envoy an audience.

"I must win him over. Cecil tells me he doesn't believe I would seriously consider any match," she says, pacing around her privy chamber. We observe her fretting. It's hard to tell when she wants us to contribute.

"I doubt it would take much effort for you, Your Grace," Lady Catherine Knollys makes the first attempt.

The queen lets out a sigh. "I worry I've refused him one too many times."

"But what would he not do for a chance to cement an alliance between two great nations?" I say.

"True," the queen says, rewarding me with a wry smile. "He should be the one courting me. But alas, this is the game I have to play."

A lady strumming the lute nearly drops her instrument. The queen snaps at her to be careful, when an idea dawns on her.

"Ah. Now I have it." She comes forward and plucks the lute from the unsuspecting lady's fingers. As the queen practises, she motions with a tilt of her head for Mary Sidney to come closer.

The following day, the envoy is led to an inner chamber to meet with her, only to discover a beautiful tableau has been prepared instead. Two columns of white flowers frame the entrance. Brilliant Turkish carpets line the floor, and at the centre of it all is the queen, playing the lute. She doesn't look up as he walks in and we invite him to sit on a cushion by her feet.

As the last notes of the song drift away, she blinks as if coming out of a trance and looks surprised to find him a supplicant at her feet.

"Very well played, Your Majesty. You are enchanting," the envoy says.

The queen giggles and offers him her hand. "You seek merely to flatter me."

"No. To hear you play is a great pleasure."

Her lashes flutter. "Do you believe the archduke will be able to tolerate my playing?"

"He would be mesmerised," the envoy says without hesitation. Queen Elizabeth is pleased with the response and takes up the lute once more. As she begins another song, she glances towards him, as coy as a fox. "Then he must come hear me play."

After a brief pause, the envoy smiles. "He will come the moment he hears you wish to marry him."

The queen laughs. "Oh, how I wish it were that simple. But what I wish for has little bearing on my decisions."

Standing by the door, I spot Robert Dudley rounding the corner, accompanied by ten men. I can see why there's a growing resentment towards him at court. His presumption certainly knows no bounds. Among the crowd, I spot Thomas Blount.

Over the last few days, I've learned he's a widower, a few years older than myself. As a distant relative of the

Dudley family, he has always served them and began his career as a pageboy for Robert's father, the Duke of Northumberland. If I hadn't run into him before, he'd be easily lost in the crowd. Now, however, I find my gaze keeps drifting towards him.

Objectively, there's nothing striking about him. He's neither handsome nor ugly. His blonde hair is still thick, and he keeps his full beard trimmed short. He exudes an air of calm dignity as he waits. When he catches me watching him, and he returns the look with a tight smile.

He's not pleased to be here either. We all know the queen does not want to be disturbed, yet here is Robert Dudley, clearly intent on interrupting this private audience.

Dudley has a word with the Yeomen of the Guard. Then at last they let him through. I'm not about to stand between him and the queen if her own guards won't.

I share an incredulous look with Thomas, who merely shrugs.

From my spot at the entrance of the doorway, I see the way Dudley struts towards the queen, head held high and completely unapologetic.

The envoy glares at the intruder, waiting for the queen to rebuke him. Instead, she invites him to sit beside her.

"Shall we sing something for you, ambassador?" the queen asks, her eyes never leaving Dudley's.

"Certainly," comes the expected response.

The queen plays, and she and Dudley sing a duet together. It's beautifully done. They both have a natural talent that practice alone could not have taught them. It would've been a pleasure for them to keep singing, but after the first song ends, the ambassador excuses himself.

"Your Majesty, I'm afraid I'm unwell and overly tired. Thank you for meeting with me today. I shall write to my master and inform him how eager you are to hear from him."

She nods.

Then it is only her and Robert left alone in the indoor pavilion of flowers. He stands and plucks flowers down from the wall and showers her with petals. She laughs and scolds him, but doesn't send him away.

Cecil arrives just in time to witness this. He turns to Kat Ashley, who pulls him aside to whisper in his ear. I cannot hear what they say, but he's clearly upset.

His face is stern as he marches into the room and asks to speak to the queen alone.

There's a tense moment as we wait to see if she will choose to listen to him. But before the queen can say anything, Robert bows and says, "I must go make sure everything is ready for tonight's banquet."

The queen dismisses him with a smile. With a cheeky grin to Cecil, Dudley retreats out of the room. Yet, this doesn't feel like a victory for Cecil. Rather, it appears as though Robert has given him permission to have this private audience. Day by day he grows bolder. But what can he hope to gain? Even if the queen would marry him, he is a married man.

"Dorothy, may I speak to you?" his voice is a gentle caress.

I have avoided Pickering for a few days, but my luck has come to an end.

Taking a step away from him, I don't even turn to look at him as I say, "there is nothing to speak about."

In the centre of the room, acrobats juggle fruit, throwing them high into the air. A laugh goes up as they all come tumbling down, pelting the poor acrobats. Then one performs a graceful leap and is lifted up on the other's shoulders.

"Please don't be cruel. I must explain myself." Pickering is persistent.

"We are acquaintances. You don't owe me an explanation. If anything, I kept pushing you away," I say, primly.

"She means nothing to me. A moment of weakness, that is all," he whispers.

"Does she know that?" I turn my head just slightly so I can catch his guilty expression. With a curt nod, I join the crowd in applauding as the acrobat performs a flip in the air from such a great height. "I am serious when I say that I am not hurt by your actions. Let this matter rest. I don't know why you pursue me so relentlessly."

"One might think you'd be flattered," he says, with a sharp edge to his voice.

"I've seen too much of the world to let myself be led by emotion so easily," I reply coolly. The lie leaves a bitter taste in my mouth. Of course, if I had truly not cared, I wouldn't have run from him that night. Nor would I be dreading this conversation. I'm not the ice queen I pretend to be.

"Then we can still be friends," he presses.

We come to it at last. The reason he's been pursuing me so relentlessly is that he values me for the information and access I can give him to the queen. I should be flattered he thinks me worth his time.

"Certainly. And as a friend, I should warn you the queen will be very displeased if she discovers you have a lover. She will see it as a betrayal."

He nods, his lips pursed. His eyes look as if he's in deep thought. Not wishing to continue this conversation, I take his momentary distraction to slip away.

Lady Catherine Knollys slips into my room that evening, her face pale.

"What is it?" I sit up, pulling on a gown over my petticoat and chemise. I was preparing for bed, not visitors.

"The Duke of Norfolk has had a public argument with Robert Dudley."

"What?" Even from here, I can see her hand shaking as she takes a seat. "I don't know what will happen if things continue on like this."

"Tell me what happened," I say, urging her for information.

"Before they entered the banquet, Robert Dudley stepped in front of the duke."

I scoff. The Duke of Norfolk is a proud man from an even prouder family, related to the queen by blood. He would have seen Dudley's presumption as a capital offense.

"The duke commanded Dudley to step back. When Dudley refused, he went on to lecture him on the order of precedence. Dudley merely laughed and said, if it was a matter of rank, then he, Dudley, ought to go first."

I gasp. "He didn't?"

Catherine Knollys puts a hand to her lips. "It was a catastrophe in the making. The Swedish envoy was witness to this too." She clears her throat. "That's not even the worst of it. The duke accused Dudley of interfering with matters of state. When Robert asked him to explain himself, the duke said outright that Robert was working to undermine every marriage proposal the queen received. He accused Dudley of wanting to marry the queen himself."

I was aghast.

"Naturally, Dudley pointed out that he was already married. This made the duke sneer and say that he'd heard Dudley had applied to have the marriage annulled, though he was sure if that failed Dudley would think of another way to rid himself of his wife. The duke went on to say such terrible things. If they had been carrying swords, I'm sure it would've come to blows. The only reason there wasn't a duel was because the queen arrived and the feast began."

"And did she hear about it?" My heart is pounding in my chest.

"She was told, but that didn't stop her from having Dudley sit on her right with the duke on her left throughout the banquet. When the Duke of Norfolk suggested she find a better dinner companion, she merely laughed. The queen spent the evening playing mediator between the two men while they fought to win her favour."

"Was there any clear victor?"

Catherine shook her head.

I bite my lower lip. "The queen knows how to play one side against the other. She does it with her suitors, and now she's doing it with her courtiers. But this is dangerous. The whole court, and by now I'm sure all of Europe, knows how much the queen admires Lord Robert. They will think she is colluding with him to put his wife aside. It would be a scandal."

"I know," Catherine whispers. "I have written to my husband to come to court as soon as he can. She has listened to him in the past. I have no idea what Cecil and Walsingham are doing about this. Really she shouldn't have let Robert talk to a duke like that. It breaks all rules of etiquette."

"Not to mention it creates more enemies for him."

A week later in the early hours of the morning, a letter arrives from a member of my aunt's household. Inside is the news I've been dreading to hear. My aunt has died. Along with the note came a letter from the executor of her will. She has left me ten pounds, two of her gowns, and the pansy brooch she once lent to me. This will be sent along to me once all her debts were paid. As a duchess, she will be interned in the Howard vault near Lambeth. As per her wishes, she will not be buried beside her long-estranged husband.

That day the court goes into half-mourning to honour her. I am excused from my duties and spend the morning praying in the queen's chapel. Because of this, I miss another great commotion in the queen's household.

Kat Ashley, worrying for the queen, took it upon herself to admonish her old charge. She pleaded with the queen to send Robert Dudley away from court to save her reputation and urged her to marry soon. The queen yelled at the poor old woman but stopped short of ordering her removed from court. In the end, she thanked Kat Ashley for the warning. But as far as I can see, nothing has changed.

When the queen is not entertaining ambassadors, reading, or responding to letters and attending privy council meetings, she is with Robert.

As Master of the Horse, he arranges an endless stream of entertainment for her, and she relishes the excitement.

We are enjoying a picnic in the woods. Carpets have been laid out on the ground and a large tent erected for the occasion. There's also a makeshift stage, and actors are preparing to put on a play. I am wandering around on the outskirts, shamelessly avoiding the gossiping ladies and intensity of the court. My mind drifts from one concern to another. I'm picking at the foliage when I spot Sir Thomas Blount approaching.

"Condolences on the loss of your aunt," Thomas Blount says with a bow of his head.

"Thank you. I know I was lucky to have had her in my life for as long as I did, but it still hurts to know she is no longer here." I find my eyes pricking with fresh tears, and I take a moment to dab at them.

He touches my arm lightly but doesn't linger. "You were close to her. It's natural you should mourn her."

A low laugh escapes my lips. "You certainly know a lot about me. Am I being spied on?"

He flushes. "No, of course not. My lord instructed me to learn the names of the queen's ladies-in-waiting but nothing else. I simply noticed ever since your aunt's death you've been melancholic. I wished to express my sympathies for your loss for some time, but didn't have the opportunity to do so."

"Did you fear being discovered?" I teased.

"The court is ripe with scandal. The courtiers are hounds looking for anything to sink their teeth into."

He has an amusing turn of phrase. I glance at him sideways, appreciating the way the sunlight has given his hair a golden sheen.

"We would make a meagre meal. Not that there's anything to be worried about."

He gives a shake of his head. "You've seen what the court is like. The truth doesn't matter."

"Perhaps, but what about your master? What is he thinking, behaving the way he has been?" I can tell from the look in his eye that he is ready with a denial but I press on. "We've seen them together. You cannot deny that if he could, he would put himself forward as a husband for her."

"No. On that point, we can both agree. But the rumours being spread about him are..."

"Close to the truth," I finish for him.

He laughs. "I didn't expect to be interrogated by you."

"What did you expect?" Now I'm the one being coy.

"That we would commiserate together over our losses and get to know each other."

I raise an eyebrow at his forward declaration. "Are you interested in me? It certainly seems so."

We are at eye-level, so nothing escapes me. His eyes crinkle with amusement. He takes up my challenge without hesitation. "Yes."

I am taken aback, though I should've expected him to answer me in this straightforward way of his. We are now behind the stage, and I witness one of the actors fighting with the laces of his gown. I hide a smile behind my hand. "Do you think I should go help him with that?"

He follows the direction of my gaze. "No. How else will he learn?"

Another actor shouts at him and comes forward to help him.

"Why are you interested in me?" I ask.

"You jump from topic to topic, seeking to catch me unaware, and leave me fumbling over my words."

I don't deny it.

"I am beginning to suspect Sir Francis Walsingham has taught you the art of questioning witnesses."

"It doesn't seem to be working," I say with a sigh. "I've barely got anything useful out of you."

"I thought we had a lot in common. That is why I found myself constantly drawn to you."

"Because we've both been widowed?"

"And you are reserved yet as sharp-tongued and witty as any of them. You strike me as the sort of woman I'd like to get to know more."

"Even if I were to inform you that despite my illustrious lineage, I haven't a penny to my name? As you can see, I must carve out a living for myself and my family at court."

"Yet another similarity we share. I think with time we could become close friends."

He waits for me to be outraged at the familiarity with which he spoke to me or declare that I want to be more than just friends. But I don't fall into the trap he has laid out for me. Rather I give him a coquettish smile and don't disagree with him.

"You'll have to excuse me, but duty calls," I say, inclining my head as I hear them announce that the play is about to begin.

"I hope we will see more of each other."

"Where my mistress goes, your master isn't far behind. I'm sure there will be several opportunities for more... conversations."

I hurry to my seat beside Lady Catherine Knollys,

who smiles at me. "I'm happy to see you in good humour again."

"On a day like this, it would be hard not to smile."

She laughs. "Yes. Well, I for one am glad that the queen is not the only one being courted."

I nudge her with my elbow. "This is hardly the time to discuss this." I am aware of the keen ears eager for gossip surround us. "I will, god willing, never leave the queen's service."

"You just need the right inducement."

"Believe me, nothing could. I value my independence too much."

She shrugs as though she doesn't believe me.

CHAPTER 10

"Your Majesty, this is serious. You cannot go through the streets accepting presents from people," Cecil says, sounding exasperated.

"The people love me. I nurture their love by going among them." The queen shakes her head. "What you are suggesting would build greater distance between myself and them. Do you think they would love me so much if I hid behind my castle walls?"

"You must take greater care," Sir Francis Walsingham says, stepping forward.

He's a soft-spoken man, a peculiar trait given his profession. His dark eyes dart around the room to make sure we are all paying attention. "We've received word from an agent at the French court that Mary of Guise is planning to have you poisoned."

The queen might scoff, but I can see the tremor in her hand. She's afraid, though she doesn't wish to show it. Robert Dudley standing behind her places a comforting hand on her shoulder. She covers it with her own as if wishing above all else to hold it there forever.

"What do you propose, then?" the queen says more seriously.

"You allow us to inspect every gift you receive. There are powders that could be sprinkled on items like clothing, or flowers. Sharp needles dipped in poison can be hidden in jewellery. It would only take one prick, and you would die," Sir Francis, lists coolly. "Your food is always tasted for poison before it is served to you. However, it is up to you to ensure you don't eat food from unknown sources."

I shudder at the thought of how easily it would be to assassinate the queen. My own anxiety is mounting, and as I glance around me at the other assembled ladies, I can see from their grave expressions that they are feeling the same.

"You see," Cecil says. "This is why I must ask Your Grace not to go out after Mass. Last summer when you were on progress, you stopped in a town and entered the home of a layman, ate their bread and cheese. It was a wonderful gesture that warmed the hearts of many, but it is far too dangerous for you to continue in this way."

The queen lets out a frustrated sigh. "No matter what I do or where I am, my life is always in danger. I cannot remember a time in my life when I felt safe," she tuts. "The court is merely filled with rumour and strife. They've grown bored and are looking for something to entertain them. All anyone can seem to talk about is strange illnesses, poison, and people being murdered."

Dudley's smile becomes strained. The queen is, of course, referring to the rumours that he is plotting to have his wife killed. No matter what he has tried to do, they will not be squashed. He received a report last week from her friends that she has been unwell, and while he wrote letters to her and urged her to see a physician, he dared not even pay her a visit.

If he saw her or sent someone to her and she died a few days later, then people would see it as proof he murdered her.

Personally, I feel appalled by his behaviour. My heart aches for the poor woman eclipsed by the queen. I wouldn't be surprised if she were to die of a broken heart. By all accounts, Amy Dudley is a sweet, caring woman who has been a loyal wife to Dudley, even when he was imprisoned by Queen Mary. The only fault she seems to possess is that she has no ambition for court politics and that she is not a queen herself. I know the match was made in haste and out of love. At the time the Dudley family was rising in power and Robert could've made a grander marriage. Were they happy in those early days? What happened between them? Did power corrupt Dudley as it had so many other men? It was possible.

It might be ungenerous of me, but I wonder if he would be so loving and attentive to the queen if she was just a gentlewoman from the country. Does she think of this, and if she does, why doesn't she send him away or keep him at arm's length?

Sir Francis Walsingham finishes listing the other ways the queen could be exposed to danger. "Your safety is paramount. We have increased the number of guards around you, but you and your ladies will also have to play your parts."

I see my own despondent expression mirrored in Catherine Knollys'.

Blanche Parry, the most senior lady, gets to her feet. "We shall do everything we can to protect the queen."

Sir Francis Walsingham gives her an approving nod.

Cecil clears his throat and the queen turns to him, but seems to know where all of this is heading. "I would be remiss if I didn't bring up the matter of your marriage. Should anything—God forbid—happen to Your Majesty, there will be nothing to stand in the way of a succession crisis and civil war. Either Spain or France would swallow us up. You must marry."

The queen gets to her feet, pushing Robert away. "Do you think I am unaware of my duty? It haunts me day and night. I am doing everything in my power to safeguard this kingdom. You and every one of my councillors urge me to marry, but that presents a fresh set of problems. What if I die in childbirth and the child with me? We would be right back to where we started. The matter of who my husband should be is even more complicated." She stops, putting a hand to her forehead. "I tire of having this conversation over and over again. There is Katherine Grey standing there, whom I could adopt as my daughter, and then we could be done with all this."

We all glance at Katherine Grey, who is keeping her eyes fixed on her lap. From my seat, I can make out the hint of a smile on her features.

"If Your Majesty would declare these intentions to parliament, I am sure it would go a long way to easing the minds of your people."

"Nonsense," she said. "That is a trap I will not fall into. After my sister declared me her heir at the urging of her husband, everyone flocked to me and tried to urge me into plots to depose her."

Cecil looks to be at his wits end. He can barely maintain his composure as what she says sinks in. "Your grace, you claim one thing and then another. You seem unable to decide on a course of action."

"Because there isn't one that I can take with any certainty. You are dismissed, Sir William," she says coldly.

He is taken aback, but he can't do anything else but retreat and leave with Sir Francis Walsingham.

The mood in the room is tense. The queen reaches for Robert, and he comes forward as though he were about to take her into his arms and never let her go.

"Your majesty, might a walk in the gardens cheer you?" Kat Ashley asks, interrupting them.

"Yes. That sounds lovely. Robert, will you accompany us?" she asks, as if there could be any doubt.

"If Your Grace wishes. I am yours to command. Always."

She smiles at him, but the smile doesn't quite reach her eyes.

∾

I am strolling through the palace's inner courtyard when my lazy meandering is interrupted by Master Hentzner, the German envoy. Against the bright green foliage and bright colours of the marigolds, he is a dark shadow swathed in heavy black velvet. He looks up and doesn't seem surprised to find me here. Perhaps he planned to run into me. It's not unheard of for foreign dignitaries to have spies set around the queen. Determined to be polite, I nod my head in greeting, ready to walk past. He stops me with a motion of his hand.

"Lady Dorothy, how do you do?" Master Hentzner asks, falling into step beside me, his smile bright.

"I am well, thank you, Master Hentzner," I say formally.

"You must call me Hans," he says, offering me his arm.

I hesitate a moment before taking it.

"I have heard many things about you from the former German envoy," he begins, leading me back up the path I had been strolling on.

"I'm surprised I'm worth mentioning in any capacity," I say with false meekness, hoping he doesn't notice the way my chest puffs out with pride.

"A lady as widely travelled as yourself is a novelty," he muses. His eyes study me closely. "Add to that your lineage and the fact that you hold the queen's favour. It is no mystery you are known to those far and wide."

I chuckle, patting his hand. "Now you seek to flatter me. I am on my guard."

He grins. "Has it worked?"

"Of course," I say, lightly. "If you continue in this vein, I believe we shall become the best of friends." I lean closer to him to say, "I ventured out here hoping to cure my headache. Where the fresh air has failed, you have succeeded."

"I am happy to hear that."

We have finished walking the perimeter of the knot garden and stop once more in front of the marigolds.

"I must return to my duties," I say, excusing myself.

"Never a moment's rest." He smiles, though his expression looks strained. "Keep me in your thoughts. I find I am often forgotten among the glitter and glamour of the others at court. It isn't easy being constantly overlooked."

I pity him, though I do my best not to let myself show it. Something about his manner and appearance reminds me of John Calvin and without meaning to, I warm considerably to him.

"Duty pulls the queen in all directions, but she would never neglect a guest," I say, barely holding back from promising to help in any sort of concrete way.

He bows his head. "She is a most gracious host."

As I return to the queen's apartments, I make a mental note to mention him when I can.

A gift of a gold bracelet appears in my chambers the following day, with a note from Master Hentzner thanking me for indulging him. There's a niggling feeling

THE LADY OF FORTUNE

in my chest as I examine the fine craftsmanship. It feels like a bribe, but I have agreed to nothing.

"I tire of being cooped up all day," the queen declares as we help her get dressed. "Lent is over yet there have been no entertainments, or masques of any kind. Just feast after feast. I need the fresh air."

"Perhaps, Sir Robert will organise a hunt," I suggest, then find myself compelled to add. "There are plenty of newcomers to court that have yet to experience the pleasures of our English forests and hunts."

The queen's sharp black eyes slid over me as she weighs my words. Still unused to how she might react, I grasp my hand to keep from fidgeting. The quiet in the room grows uncomfortable, but at last she says, "send for him."

I bow and rush to do as she bids.

The following day the sky overhead is blue and a large hunting party is preparing to ride out. Among the crowd I notice the German envoy and I hope he is pleased to be included. The queen is at the forefront in a dazzling cream velvet gown covered in delicate green embroidery.

William Cecil is watching the queen with unconcealed concern. He's not alone in his worry. I've been witness to many councillors petitioning her to curtail her wilder pastimes. After all, a fall from a horse, or a misfired crossbow, would cause the end of her line and plunge the country into chaos. Much to their chagrin, their concerns continue to fall on deaf ears. I watch as she spurns her horse forward, Robert Dudley hot on her heels. The sound of hooves on cobblestone and the baying of hounds fills the air as we follow them.

Two hours later, a stag is cornered. The hounds are hard to hold back and their yipping and snarls fill the forest. Once the animal is secure they invite the queen to deal the killing blow. Her movements are swift and sure, and thankfully the sounds of the struggling creature cease. We all applaud as she is helped back into the saddle.

With the business done we turn our horses to ride for a pavilion. The stag is left to the servants to carry back to the palace, where it will be prepared for tomorrow's banquet.

At the pavilion, the mood runs high from today's success. I am refilling the queen's goblet when I spy Master Hentzner from the corner of my eye. Musicians strike up a tune and someone says a bawdy joke that sends all the men laughing. I take the opportunity to whisper to the queen and she looks over in envoy's direction. With a graceful movement of her wrist, she invites him to come forward.

"Welcome Master Hentzner," she says, as if she's known who he was all this time. "I hope you enjoyed the hunt and didn't find it too exhausting for you."

"Not at all, Your Majesty. It was a glorious day. I am honoured..."

Before he can say more, Robert Dudley comes up to the dais and the queen is distracted.

Master Hentzner is forced to bow and retreat. His eyes flash with displeasure. I am sure there was more he wished to say. With a sigh, I try to avoid looking in his direction.

Three days later I am tucked away in a forgotten corridor at the palace of Westminster, practicing my lines for a masque when he approaches me.

"Good day," I say, greeting him with a friendly smile.

His expression remains withdrawn. "What is going on?"

I look down at my gown of blue and green gauze. "I am to be a nymph, but I have yet to remember my lines. Tomorrow the entire court will celebrate Saint George's Day..."

"Not that." He shuffles closer. "When will I be given another audience with the queen?"

"What do you mean?" I say, straightening up. It comes to my attention that I am quite isolated here, though I could hardly imagine he means to harm me.

"You were meant to put in a good word for me. To help me with her majesty. It's imperative I see her."

I stiffen. "We never agreed on anything. I have no idea what you mean," I say, raising my voice in the hope someone would overhear and come to investigate.

He guffaws. "You think I'd just give a gold bracelet to just anyone?"

"I took it as a gift. If you wish to have it back, I will be more than happy to return it to you."

He scowls, ready to say something when Sir Thomas Blount rounds the corner. He stops short when he sees us.

"Good day, Master," he says, his tone impassive as he

tries to assess the situation he's stumbled upon. "May I be of some assistance?"

Master Hentzner regards him coolly. "We were discussing something private."

Sir Thomas' gaze falls on me for a moment. "It doesn't seem the lady is comfortable. Have you threatened or attempted to assault a Lady of the Bedchamber?" His accusation is cutting and makes the envoy's jaw drop.

"N-no!" he sputters, his eyes wide with outrage.

"Then I suggest you leave. What business could you have here?"

Hentzner looks like he wants to argue, but then spins on his heel and stalks back the way he came. Once he is out of sight, Sir Thomas turns to me with an eyebrow raised as he waits for my explanation.

"He wasn't lying. He didn't harass me, but I was beginning to fear he might the more upset he got."

"I heard raised voices," Sir Thomas says. "I'm glad I came to investigate."

"I am as well." Then with some amusement I add, "that's twice now you've helped me or tried to anyway. I suppose I should regard you as my very own hero."

He grins, "I would be flattered if you did. What are you doing here all alone?"

"Practicing for tomorrow. I'm to play the part of a nymph. One of many stolen by the dragon."

"Ah and will Saint George ride to your rescue?"

"Something like that. You will have to wait to see. I fear I've already spoiled too much," I say.

He looks as though he's about to say something but instead catches himself. Clearing his throat, he says, "I'll leave you to it then. Good luck, Lady Dorothy."

The celebration for Saint George's Day is a success. It is late by the time we retire for the evening. As the queen climbs into her bed, she calls me to her side.

"Yes, Your Grace?" I say, coming up from my curtsey.

"I wish for you to deliver a message to Sir Robert for me. Then she adds, "in secret. No one else must know."

My hand drifts to the gold chain around my neck. I twist the locket between my fingers. I stare up at the gilded ceiling wondering how on earth such a thing could be accomplished?

"I shall try, Your Grace."

She fixes me with a look that warns me not to disappoint her. Her hands smooth over the quilts of brilliant silk covering her bed. "I have every faith you will see it done." She slips a rolled-up piece of parchment into my hand. "He will know it's from me."

In the privacy of my room, I'm wringing my hands together, unsure how she expects me to do this. I must have a plausible reason for entering Dudley's rooms. In the end, I call Catherine into my room.

"You want me to do what?" She laughs incredulously as I lay out my plan.

"Dress me like a scullery maid. I'll be able to move around the palace with no one being the wiser."

"There are other ways you can meet someone in secret if that is your goal," she says with barely contained mirth. "Think of the amount of times Mary Sidney has snuck out with messages in the dead of night," she says.

"That's exactly why I cannot do as she did. Someone would know. Will you help me or not?"

"Fine. I suppose I must help you," she says, eyeing me suspiciously. "You aren't meeting with a lover, are you? Such a risk to your reputation..." she trails off.

I straighten up, a look of outrage on my face. "I believe I was once your stepmother, not the other way around. Don't seek to school me in good manners. Rest assured, I'm not doing this to meet a lover."

"Apologies," she says, but from her tone it's not clear she believes me or not. Regardless, she does help me.

The next morning, before the first signs of dawn, I am dressed in the plain garb of a serving wench. The rough wool scratches me through my fine linen shift. I scratch at my neck and pull at the tight sleeves. Catherine ties the cap in place. "Are you sure about this?"

I can think of no better way. With a shrug, I thank her one last time and slip out of my room. Carrying my message tucked into the sleeves of the gown as I lug my woven basket of kindling.

A man is guarding the door to Robert Dudley's apartments. Keeping my head down, I reach for the door handle.

"You aren't allowed to enter," he says gruffly.

I give a nonchalant shrug though my heart hammers in my chest. "Doesn't matter to me. I was ordered to come."

He studies me closer.

I turn to leave when he stops me.

"Ordered? By who?"

"Some lord, I don't know. He merely wanted a fire lit in Lord Dudley's rooms," I say doing my best to impersonate a servant.

His eyebrow arches in disbelief. I can tell he's about to send me away, so in a moment of desperation I say, "His name was Blount."

He hesitates, then finally admits me. "Be quick about it. I'll remember you if anything goes missing."

"Yes, sir."

Once inside with the door closed behind me, I face a new problem. How do I get to Dudley? I can't barge into his bedchamber. As I'm trying to puzzle the door opens behind me. With a start, I rush over to the fireplace and kneel before it.

When I hear the door shutting again, I dare to peek over my shoulder.

Sir Thomas Blount is standing there, hands on his hips, as he regards me with a mixture of incredulity and exasperation.

"I must be dreaming because I cannot be seeing Lady Dorothy here in my lord's rooms."

"Shh." I try to hush him, getting to my feet. He walks over, taking in my disguise and the kindling abandoned on the floor.

"I should let you continue on with your work then," he says.

I roll my eyes. "I was sent here in secret with a message for your master."

"Of course, you were. What I'm trying to determine is why you went to such lengths..."

I let out a frustrated growl. "Please spare me your mockery. May I see Sir Robert? I have to deliver a message into his hands and no one else's. Not that I'd trust you."

He places a hand over his heart as if I've wounded him.

"This is not a jest," I say.

"You are right." Sir Thomas can barely keep from smiling. Then his face grows more serious. "Why should I let you deliver your message? I assume it's from the queen."

"And to think of how close we've grown. I can see I was wrong about you. You aren't a chivalric knight."

"I also doubt you are a damsel in distress. You seem quite capable of handling whatever the world throws at you."

I blink, taken aback by the change in his tone. Slowly, I realise he meant for it to be a compliment.

Licking my lips, I try to reason with him again. "Will you not help me? I don't like to leave a task unfinished."

"Very well, Lady Dorothy. Perhaps, next time you might feel comfortable enough to come to me directly without putting on such a theatrical display."

I grin triumphantly. "I believe that is a fair compromise."

He leaves to fetch his master while I stand there wondering at my sudden hope our paths shall cross once again.

CHAPTER 11

Rumours have spread far and wide that the queen is planning to adopt Katherine Grey and naming her the heir to the English throne. There's a marked difference in the respect courtiers show her. Katherine certainly walks around the court with an extra skip to her step. However, tragedy strikes when an urgent message arrives informing that her mother has passed away in her sleep.

We knew that the countess had been sick for quite some time, but no one thought she would die so suddenly and without warning. The queen orders her a grand state funeral, and the whole court is to wear black.

Cleverly, Queen Elizabeth also uses this as an excuse to avoid discussing her marriage. However, we all note wryly that her sadness doesn't prevent her from continuing to ride out every day with Dudley nor from attending a joust the following day. Dudley rides in the lists carrying her favour, and she applauds him as he beats one challenger after another.

There is no one else for her but him.

By now, we've all learned to be silent when it comes to Robert Dudley. So we look the other way as day by day, he grows more familiar and is showered with more honour and wealth.

For once I feel myself pitying Lady Katherine Grey, who appears to be shaken by the death of her mother. Her friend, Lady Jane, is ill with coughing fits that don't seem to abate no matter what she does.

I approach them while they are sewing by a bay window, intent on offering my sincere condolences when I catch a few words of their conversation.

"She promised to ask the queen for me," Katherine says with a small sob. "But she never got the chance to. What will I do now?"

"I am here. I know..." Jane catches sight of me and stiffens.

Pretending I heard nothing, I approach, a book of prayers extended in my hand.

"I find reading them helps me make sense of tragedy," I say, offering the tiny leather-bound book to her. "It isn't much, but I hope it can help ease your sorrows."

Katherine wipes the tears from her eyes and has the graciousness to thank me. But I can't help but notice the look of disdain that passes between the two young ladies.

∽

On a golden autumn day, the queen names Dudley as Lord Commander of Windsor Castle, an honour that carries with it more wealth and prestige for him.

Pamphlets deriding him appear in London, and the queen orders the printers to be arrested.

"You must pardon them," Dudley says. We can all hear the urgency in his voice.

She is playing the virginals in her presence chamber. The sun is dipping low as servants move around the room lighting lamps and candles.

"Why should I? They are printing scandalous gossip about one of my most trusted courtiers. I won't put up with it."

"The people hate me enough as it is. They will blame me for the deaths of these men if you continue."

"What does it matter if the people hate you?" The queen's eyes spark dangerously.

He is taken aback. At a loss for words, he merely gapes at her.

"It certainly matters to me," he whispers in an angry hiss.

I can only hear him because I am working on embroidery near the queen. My eyes find Thomas Blount standing at the far back of the room, and my eyebrows rise in silent question.

He looks away, knowing that his master is overreaching himself lately. The queen favours him above all others, but even she has limits. She never likes to have her power questioned. Or feel that others are trying to win popular opinion.

Dudley is forgetting himself as he steps towards the queen. His eyes are full of frustrated anger. She meets him step for step. They are either going to come to blows or embrace each other passionately.

"Perhaps my lord has forgotten, but he told the Spanish ambassador he might have a tour of the queen's stables so he could pick a mount for tomorrow's hunt," I interject before either of them says something they will regret.

That checks him and the queen. They both take a step back from each other.

"Yes, Lady Dorothy," he says, straightening his sleeve. "It has slipped my mind. Do I have your permission to go, Your Grace?" he turns to the queen with a respectful bow.

"Yes. I am tired and should rest."

"May I see you later?" he whispers.

She considers him for a moment, then nods. Satisfied, he leaves the room. I catch Thomas lingering by the doorway. It's flattering to think he might be unwilling to leave because of me. But then he is gone.

As silence descends on the room, we all hear Jane Seymour wracked by another coughing fit.

"Perhaps, you should go rest, Lady Jane," the queen says to her in a kind tone.

Katherine Grey helps her friend to her feet, and the two plod away.

"Lady Dorothy, will you attend me?" the queen says, retreating to her privy chamber. With some surprise, I get to my feet and hurry after her.

As the weather grows colder, Robert Dudley arranges one last tournament before winter sets in.

The queen sits in a pavilion covered by red and white roses. On either side of her sit the envoys from Spain and Sweden. She speaks to both of her longing for marriage and a husband to help ease her troubles.

They listen to her with rapt attention. She certainly knows how to capture their attention.

All the while, I realise her attention is on the jousts below. The Duke of Norfolk will ride against Robert Dudley soon. I wonder who was bribed to make this come about.

The queen might have been given a proper chair to sit on, but we ladies have to make do with cushions on benches. After a few hours of sitting, I find my legs falling asleep, and I excuse myself to go stretch.

The queen's Yeomen of the Guard are assembled around the stage to protect her, and one offers his hand to help me down the last step. I am intent on taking a quick stroll and returning to my position when I see that Sir Thomas Blount close by, sitting among the crowd.

As if sensing me watching him, he looks up. He smiles and makes his way over to me.

"How do you do, Lady Dorothy?" He doffs his cap.

"I am well. You didn't have to come speak to me. You will miss the next round."

"I am certain it shall be much the same as the last one. There will be a man in heavy armour riding a horse on either end, and they shall charge, hoping to knock one other down."

"You sound like you don't enjoy the sport."

Sheepishly, he shrugs. "It can be quite repetitive. But perhaps, I would like it more if I could afford to partake." His breath is coming out in heavy clouds of mist. The air feels colder here than in the protected embrace of the tent walls. He rubs his hands together. "And in weather like this, I find I grow cold." He laughs at himself. "I've become an old man griping about the weather. I should be busy impressing you with my prowess."

"I appreciate the honesty. If you must know, I felt my legs falling asleep and couldn't stand sitting for another moment. Neither of us are in our prime any longer."

He scoffs. "Nonsense. You are a handsome woman."

"If you think so." I flash him a smile. "You certainly are full of compliments today."

With a shrug, he offers me his arm. I surprise myself by taking it.

"Shall we take a quick stroll before I am forced to return you back to the queen?"

I nod. "The last we spoke, you refused to speak about the relationship between your master and the queen. Are you still?"

"There is nothing for me to say. I suspect you already can guess my own thoughts, and I would bet they mirror your own."

"His wife—is she truly sick, or is that just another rumour?"

"I'm afraid she is ill. Lord Robert is beside himself with how to help her."

"I thought they were estranged."

"He pays court to the queen, and of course he is enchanted with her. Who wouldn't be by such a powerful monarch? But he's not as faithless as others make him out to be."

I look more closely at him. His jaw is set tight, as though he's holding back from saying something more unsavoury. "You are right. I don't believe you'd be the sort of man to stay in the employ of someone you don't respect."

"A very astute observation. I am pleased to be growing in your esteem day by day."

"In a court like this, you are a rarity."

"Oh?"

I flush. He has a way of getting me to feel at ease and speak frankly with him. I pull the furred cape tighter around me. "There are many with fewer scruples than you. I find your honesty refreshing."

"Here I thought being handsome and brave was all that was required to capture the attention of a lady. I should write out a pamphlet so men everywhere can be alerted to this new discovery," he says, teasing.

"Who says you've managed to capture my attention?" As we round the bend, the wind blows fiercely and leaves me shivering fiercely.

We stop, and he takes my hands in his, bringing them to his lips. I watch incredulously as he places a kiss on my gloved fingertips. He regards me with such intensity; it makes my breath hitch. We stay like that, frozen for a moment by our closeness and daring.

Then I pull away laughing. "If you seek to warm my hands, you must try harder."

"Careful, Lady Dorothy, that sounds like an invitation."

Amusement flashes across my features. "Perhaps it is, but I shall never tell you."

"You put me in an impossible position."

"How so?"

"You take one step towards me, and then you retreat. I think you've picked up the habit from the queen."

"I am a fast learner. Something of which I believe you've accused me in the past."

"True."

We've come full circle back to the queen's pavilion, and I am about to climb back up the stairs when he calls out to me. "I hope you will give me the honour of escorting you in the future."

I hesitate. The temptation to tease him is there, but instead I agree.

His smile brightens his expression. He looks ready to jump for joy as I retreat up the stairs.

The queen sees me enter. "Ah, there you are, Lady Dorothy. I was just telling Lord John how you passed through his great nation at one time. Did you not?"

I curtsey three times and rush to the queen's side. "Yes, Your Majesty." Turning to the Duke of Finland, I say, "I had the pleasure to visit your country four years ago."

He looks surprised and pleased all the same. "Wonderful country, is it not?"

"Oh, yes, I've never seen such beautiful landscapes. Though the thought of home was too much to keep me away from England."

"And the men," he grins. "Very handsome, yes?"

His English is stilted, and for this last question he's switched to Swedish. I flush pink wondering how to answer. The queen, who has not understood this last statement, looks between the two of us and waits for a translation.

"He asked me if I found the men handsome," I tell the queen, who looks amused by the bold question.

"And did you?"

"I travelled there as a married woman. I did not notice such things," I say first in English, then repeat in Swedish.

The duke guffaws. "You had eyes, did you not? Tell her majesty."

I can barely stand to look at her. "Yes, they were very pleasing to the eye."

The duke laughs and claps me on the back. The queen takes pity on me and bids me to rise to my feet. "So you think a marriage to the Prince of Sweden would be a happy one?"

"If handsomeness is the only criteria you are considering when deciding on a future husband. As I have never spent time with the prince myself, I wouldn't be able to comment on his other traits. Nor would I presume to know Your Majesty's preferences in a husband."

Her laughter fills the air. "Well put. Thank you, Lady Dorothy."

I curtsey again, and I'm almost back to my seat when she turns to me and motions me to return. She leans so close to me I can feel the edge of her ruff against my neck. "Give this to Blount. He will know what to do." As she pulls away, she slips something into my hand. It's a folded kerchief.

I take it and, without a word slip back down the stairs. Inwardly, I'm mortified that the queen must know I have some sort of relationship with him to know I could find him.

He's where I first saw him, and I try not to be too obvious as I make my way to him. Luckily, I blend in with the other women on the lower benches.

"I hadn't expected you to find me so soon," he teases, but he sees my worried expression.

"What is it?" he whispers.

"This is from the queen," I say, handing him the folded kerchief.

He doesn't seem surprised and tucks it into his pocket. "I will make sure Lord Robert gets this."

I nod. So this sort of thing is common for them. I glance up at the pavilion. What would the envoys say if they knew the queen was sending love tokens to Dudley while pretending to be interested in their matches?

"Something has distressed you."

I bite the inside of my cheek. "Is there gossip about us? How does the queen know I know you? Are people talking about us?"

He looks as though he wants to laugh. "You are jumping to conclusions. Is there anything wrong with us conversing? We've done nothing."

I grip my forearm. "A scandal wouldn't affect you. It would be easy for you to brush it aside."

"This," he says, touching his pocket, "is a sign of the queen's growing trust in you. She doesn't suspect anything is going on between us. However, I wonder why you are so worried? Do you like me, Lady Dorothy?"

If we weren't in public, I might lash out, blush and refuse to say anything.

"Tell me." He leans in closer. I feel his breath against my ear and shudder.

"Never." I pull away, knowing I've given him his answer.

For the Christmas feast, we all dress in white satin gowns and pin red silk flowers to our hair. The queen dresses in brilliant green and gold. She drips with emeralds. Half-way through the festivities, she changes into a gown of crimson red. Her eyes are lively and her mood bright. No one can take their eyes off her as she and Robert Dudley dance.

I catch the way the Duke of Norfolk watches Dudley with disgust. He drinks cup after cup of wine. I grow worried that once he is drunk, he won't be able to hold himself back.

I glance at Lady Knollys, who has noticed this as

well. Her lips purse in a tight line of displeasure as she follows the duke's progress around the room. He's not the sort of man you'd want to trifle with.

"What should we do?" I whisper to her.

"There's nothing we can do. There are plenty of guards all around. I don't think her majesty is in any danger."

"And Dudley?"

She gives me a look that says he's a different story.

"Does the queen not care that he's so hated? You'd think she would distance herself from someone so unpopular."

Lady Knollys gives a shake of her head. One of the silk roses falls loose, and I bend to pick it off the ground.

"She prefers it that way. Unless, of course, it's affecting her own popularity."

We know she wishes to be the centre of a glittering court. I glance at the queen. Given her upbringing, it's unsurprising that she would always feel the need to be the most popular, the most powerful, the most beautiful. She was born a disappointment to both her father and mother because she wasn't the son they prayed for. After they executed her mother, her position was uncertain, and she was left alone, abandoned by her father until Catherine Parr took pity on her. It must have been an uncomfortable upbringing full of uncertainty.

As the song draws to a close, the musicians strike up a country dance. We ladies are to join in, so I move to rise. My feet are throbbing from a day spent standing. I long for my bed.

Duke John of Finland approaches me with a gallant smile and offers me his hand.

Honoured, I take it and let him lead me to the other dancers, but not before I catch Sir Thomas Blount lingering at the back of the room. He raises his cup to me and takes a sip.

The whole time I'm being twirled around, I feel his rapt attention on me.

"You are a very gracious dancer," the duke says.

"It is an honour to hear you say so," I say, keeping my eyes downcast.

"And the queen, can you tell me, does she truly mean to marry my master?"

"I don't know," I say. "The queen has every intention of marrying."

"I see. Let me speak frankly, my lady. My brother wishes to sail to England and come woo the queen in person. He is the best match for her. Our kingdom might not be as grand as the Hapsburg Empire, but we are Protestant, as is her majesty. We would make a valuable alliance."

I nod politely. Surely, he must know the queen won't want my opinion, much less listen to me.

"My brother would never reproach her for Dudley. He is an understanding man. As long as Dudley is sent away from court once they are married, of course."

My lips part, incredulous. What is he saying? "I'm sorry, I don't understand, Your Grace."

The musicians take up another tune. Our conversation is interrupted by the arrival of Thomas Blount, who asks for my hand in the next dance. Wanting to get away from the Swedish envoy, I accept heartily.

"We shall speak another time, Lady Dorothy," Duke John says and retreats.

I'm still puzzling out what he said as Thomas whisks me off to join the dancers. He's an excellent partner with a natural feel for the music. I note his strength as he lifts me up into the air and lowers me down with effortless grace.

"You looked distressed," he whispers in my ear.

"We cannot speak now. Find me later?"

He nods.

As the evening drags on, many people retire. The hall is emptying, but the queen shows no signs of exhaustion.

I wait at the back of the room near a window, enjoying the cool draft coming from the windowpanes, when Thomas finally finds me again.

"You wished to speak to me," he says, coming up beside me. He is standing a respectable distance away. People might mistake us for complete strangers.

"The Swedish duke said something strange to me as we danced. He said that the prince would not mind... well, he suggested that the queen might have an unchaste relationship with your master and that the prince, having heard of it, would not mind."

Thomas's intake of breath sounds like a hiss.

"It is an old rumour," I say. "But dangerous if it is so wildly repeated."

"There's no foundation for it," he says, but it sounds more like he's trying to reassure himself.

"Would it matter? Perhaps Sir Robert should be warned to keep away from the queen. It is damaging her reputation internationally."

He gives a shake of his head. "I could not say such things to him. Not that he would listen either. The both of us serve stubborn masters."

My smile is strained as I look over towards the queen. Her cheeks are rosy with colour from all the dancing. It's then I notice the Duke of Norfolk making his way towards them.

"Oh, no."

Thomas Blount follows my gaze and curses under his breath. With a hand, he indicates I should wait here and goes forward ready to intervene.

The Duke of Norfolk bows to the queen but rudely doesn't address Robert at all. He says something to the queen, who goes pale with rage and retreats to her throne.

I cannot hear Dudley's response, but the duke lets out an explosive shout.

"You are nothing but a traitor's son!"

Quiet descends upon the court. Everyone turns to watch the scene unfolding at the centre of the dancefloor.

I catch the way Robert Dudley's hands are clenched into fists before he disappears from my view as the crowd presses forward. Will it come to blows this time?

They shout angry words back and forth. Both men look towards the queen, who is refusing to intervene.

To everyone's surprise, it is Dudley who storms off. The queen watches him go but doesn't call him back.

The duke is left standing in the centre of it all, looking victorious.

The celebratory mood has vanished. Everyone returns to their chambers for the evening, including the queen. What fresh trouble will tomorrow bring?

"What do you expect me to do?" the queen shouts at Dudley without caring who might hear her.

Far quieter, he responds, "You might have stopped him from embarrassing me. Please, be calm."

Her temper, when stoked, will not be quenched. There is a certain joy in her eyes every time she gives her councillors and favourites a dressing down, and this time is no different. "You overreach yourself."

He takes hold of her hand in a way that any other man would've been arrested for. Dudley leans in, whispering something to her, but she yanks her hand out of his grip and marches away. This leaves him in the awkward position of having to chase after her. We rush to catch up to them.

If anyone came across us, we would make an interesting tableau, but walking through the extensive palace gardens, with its high hedges and ornate arches, we are hidden from view. The queen personally selected me to be one of three ladies to accompany her. I was proud at the time, but as someone who hates conflict, I wish I wasn't here. This is a monarch and a chief official in her household. Yet, at this moment, they are acting like children.

Further behind the queen's ladies are Dudley's attendants. Among them, I know I will find Thomas. I crane my neck to glance at him wondering, what he makes of all of this.

We round the corner and find the queen has seated herself on a stone bench. Robert is on his knees before her, head hung down apologetic.

We pull back, giving them a moment of privacy.

"I only seek to serve and protect you," he says, in a low rumble.

"Then you must do better to remember that," she remonstrates him, but her eyes have softened. After a while, she places her hand on the top of his head.

He looks into her eyes with what I can only imagine is a plaintive expression.

"Sit beside me," the queen says at last. They speak with their heads together in hushed tones so we cannot hear them.

I pull back. Not knowing how long they will be like this, I take the time to admire a statue nearby. It's then Thomas Blount approaches me.

"May I speak to you?"

"Now?" I say, raising my eyebrow. "I can hardly leave my post."

"Then meet me while the queen is attending the privy council meeting today."

"Do you think I have nothing else to do with my time?"

Without even looking at him, I know he's grinning. "I'll meet you here in this garden."

I don't respond. Do I dare?

The fact I'm even considering it worries me.

At midday, I wander to the gardens. He's there waiting for me. I'm glad that he has the decency to look pleased and not triumphant. Without a word, we wander deeper into the maze and find a spot in the shade to rest.

"The queen has been in a foul temper all morning," I say to him.

"Any idea what she will do?"

I look at him through my lashes. "That information would not come cheaply."

"I am but a humble knight and have nothing to offer you. Perhaps you should sell your information to one of the foreign dignitaries."

I pretend to consider only to break out into a laugh.

"It has not gone so well for me in the past. You wished to speak to me," I say. "Is this what you wanted to ask?"

"No. I'd hoped that Dudley and the queen would've patched things up by now."

"I think the queen will side with Dudley, if that is

what you are both concerned about. She asked Cecil to discuss the state of the Scottish borders with her. That would fall under the jurisdiction of the duke, would it not?"

Thomas nods as his gaze moves over my face. "There is another reason I wished to see you. Ask me again what it is."

"I'm not in the habit of taking orders," I say.

"I'd never seek to command you."

There's that sincerity again that sends my heart soaring. With an edge of flirtation to my voice, I ask, "Why did you want me to meet you alone?"

"I was tired of having to share your attention with others," he says in a whisper, as if admitting a sinful secret.

I move closer to him, my tone teasing, as I ask, "Ah, is that all?"

Without warning, his hand reaches out, cupping my face and drawing me closer still. His lips descend upon mine, and I'm lost in a haze of passionate desire I never thought possible.

When we pull away, we are both breathless.

"I dreamed of kissing you," Thomas says. He caresses my cheek until I pull away.

"I must go," I say, touching a hand to my face.

"Stay. I promise I won't touch you again," he says. His features contort with worry.

A bitter laugh escapes me. "You are wrong to assume that I wouldn't wish to repeat that experience. But I cannot, regardless of what your intentions might be..."

He takes my hand in his. "They are the noblest of intentions. I wish to speak to you about the possibility of marriage."

Gently, I pull away. "Marriage would be impossible."

"I know I'm not wealthy. But my modest home is comfortable. I would look after you and your children from your first marriage."

"Thomas," I say, placing a hand on his forearm. "I cannot leave my place at court. Marriage is not something I ever want to enter into again. Nor could I bring myself to risk—." I pause, blushing just thinking about it. "—my reputation by becoming your mistress."

"I—" he begins, but finds himself at a loss for words.

There's no time to dwell on my daring behaviour or the kiss. The following day, William Cecil brings the queen a pamphlet being distributed in the city. Inside, it paints the queen as a malicious woman plotting to murder Amy Dudley so she may marry Robert. It's likely the work of the Spanish trying to spread discontent. But knowing who the perpetrator is doesn't stop the queen from going into a fury. There is no simple solution. Even if she were to send Dudley away from court, it wouldn't stop the wagging tongues.

The one thing that might help is something she refuses to do.

Every day her councillors arrive at her presence chamber, unrelenting in their demands that she marry.

Predictably, she assures them she will and then backtrack on her promises.

I'm working on some embroidery for the queen's petticoat when Lady Mary Glouster sits down beside me.

"Have you heard that they hanged a woman for claiming to have the queen's midwife?"

"No! Impossible," I say, my mouth hanging open. "I can't believe it."

Lady Mary pulls at her leather gloves, pleased by my reaction. Of all the queen's ladies, she is the one who most thrives on gossip and enjoys spreading it around the court. She doesn't even have the decency to be coy or demand payment. Her sources might be dubious, but her stories are no less entertaining.

"There are always rumours about the queen's chastity—or as the French and Spanish believe, the lack of it. The Pope has called her a harlot."

I shake my head in frustrated disbelief. "When will their tongues cease spreading such slander?"

"Never, at this rate," she sighs. "I suspect it will never stop, even after our mistress has married and produced an heir to England."

I clamp my mouth shut. She's egging me on in this conversation. I may say something I don't mean to.

"My lady," she says, her voice full of concern. "Are you well?"

I clear my throat. "Certainly. I am just saddened by the news of these terrible rumours. We must cast them aside and never speak of them again. It would only strengthen them if we kept discussing them."

Lady Gloucester looks disappointed, but she simply goes spread her poison elsewhere.

The queen, far from taking caution after the latest rumours, is intent on pressing on as though nothing has happened. Whatever argument she had with Robert Dudley is set aside.

We celebrate the new year with pomp and grandeur not seen in England in years. As Master of the Horse, Dudley, arranges magnificent festivities and entertainments for the queen. There is a joust, a troupe of mummers, fireworks over the Thames, and a mock battle over a marzipan castle.

There never seems to be a moment to rest.

But one day, I manage to steal into the city of London and purchase little gifts to send to my children.

I'm examining some pretty ribbon when I hear a familiar voice somewhere nearby.

"Four of those beautiful silk roses, please," Thomas Blount says.

As discreetly as possible, I turn to watch him as he pays the shopkeeper. I try to look away, but I move too slow. He's caught my attention.

"Lady Dorothy," he says, approaching. "I didn't expect to see you here today."

"Sir Thomas," I say with a small curtsey. "A pleasure."

"The pleasure is all mine," he says, capturing my hand and bringing it up to his lips. He places a chaste kiss on my gloved hand, his thumb stroking the back of my palm.

Realising I'm lingering too long, I say, "I bid you good day."

But I don't get far. In two strides he catches up to me. "My lady, you cannot expect me to let you wander the streets on your own."

"I have a maid with me, and I don't plan on venturing far—"

He cuts me off with a laugh. "Do you think that would stop the cutpurses of London from robbing you blind? Nay, lady, I insist on accompanying you."

I want to argue. After all, in the past, I've haggled over the price of fish with merchants. But I know that is not something I should brag about.

"You leave me no choice, sir," I say, unable to deny that I welcome his company. The kiss has not been forgotten. I thought I was clear that we couldn't pursue a relationship. If it is a wife he wants, shouldn't he be on the lookout for someone more amenable?

He offers me his arm, and we stroll together down the cobbled streets of London, stopping in at a shop here and there. Without a word, he carries my parcels, happy to play the part of the manservant for me.

"Who are all these for?" he asks.

"My children," I say, watching his expression, which

remains unchanged. "They are under the care of my parents. I miss them, and I wish I could've been with them this Christmas season."

"You are an unusually caring mother," he says. "My own never thought to send me gifts whenever she was away, but she loved me in her own way. I'm afraid my son is too old to appreciate little gifts from me."

"Nonetheless, I'm sure he enjoys hearing from you. Perhaps, a few coins for him to spend would be welcome," I suggest. We approach the palace, and the guards step aside to let us through.

"Thank you for your assistance today, Sir Thomas. It was unnecessary, but no less welcome."

He nods. "The pleasure was all mine. One that I hope to repeat in the future."

I blink, my lips part in surprise. "Thomas..."

But he's already gone by the time I find my voice. His coy smile is imprinted in my mind. I realise he is intent on courting me. There's been some confusion. I shall have to speak to him again.

That evening I stare in the looking glass. A handsome face stares back at me. My long hair is a thick reddish brown and my brown eyes are lively. The year I've spent at court has been good to me. Whereas before I was looking haggard, worn down by stress and financial difficulties, now I look joyful. The steady meals at court have filled out my face, and I look at ease, though serving the queen is not always easy. Perhaps it is not so unlikely that a man would appreciate my comely appearance.

Of course, none of it matters.

I swore an oath when I entered the queen's service, and I am not allowed to marry without her express permission. The queen prefers to keep her ladies-in-waiting close and isn't likely to allow me to.

Besides, is yoking myself to another man something I wish to do? No. Not even for someone as sweet and tempting as Thomas Blount.

I set aside the foolish thoughts whirling in my brain. I could blame the love poems and sonnets that are popular at court now.

Wherever I turn, I encounter romance. From the scullery maid running off to get married to the poems passed in secret to the ladies of the bedchamber. As we enter the new year, the court comes alive with hope and excitement for the future. The queen blossoms under the attention of her growing list of suitors and that passion spills over on to all of us.

That evening when we all partner up and dance to the applause of the court, I catch Thomas Blount watching me. He hesitates for the briefest moment before taking my hand and leading me into the fray. His lingering touches ignite old passions, and when he suggests we take a stroll in the moonlit courtyard, I let him pull me away.

We do nothing more than embrace and exchange sweet words of affection and admiration.

"Are you still determined not to marry me?" he asks, his finger trailing over my exposed collarbone. His touch sets my skin alight. He can see the desire in my eyes as I reach for him again.

"Quite determined," I say with conviction.

"There's no one else I would wed but you." His lips replace his fingers.

"And even if I keep refusing?"

"Then I shall have to content myself with stolen moments like these."

I bite back a moan of pleasure as his arm wraps around my middle, pulling me tightly against him.

"I should return to the hall," I say as my fingers bury themselves in his thick locks. How has he managed to enchant me so thoroughly that I'm ready to risk everything?

At last, I can no longer postpone, and I pull myself away from him.

"I must go, but we will meet again," I promise.

He holds me close. "I'll wait for you."

My eyes fixate on the pebbles at our feet. "I understand this is nothing but another game of courtly love. If there is another you want, then I understand."

He places a finger under my chin and tilts my head up so I'm looking at him. "I've married once already to please my family and have children. They no longer hold sway over me. Nothing but the deepest affection could induce me to enter into another marriage."

"I've been married before too. I'm sorry, I wish to be with you..."

"Hush. Let's not ruin this moment. Go. See to your duties. We will have other opportunities."

With a heavy heart, I return to the queen's side.

Looking out at the assembled courtiers, I realise I no

longer see them with the eyes of an ingenue. I see desperate men clambering for favour and women ready to ruin themselves. At the centre of it all is the queen. Content to watch from afar and enjoy their affections while still safeguarding her virtue.

CHAPTER 13

The queen, tired of the constant enmity between her favourite and her relative the Duke of Norfolk, makes the decision to send him away.

With a firm command, she sends the duke to safeguard the northern border. It might have been seen as a mark of her favour, but seeing the way Dudley struts around the court, it is clear to everyone that the duke was sent away at his urging.

Many find they cannot stomach Dudley's rise to greater and greater heights.

Cecil, who advised the queen against sending the duke away, finds himself sent on a diplomatic mission to sign the Treaty of Edinburgh, another honour that requires him to leave the queen's presence.

To further reward Cecil, the queen summons his son Tom and the Earl of Hertford. Both these young men, despite their lineage and the political astuteness of their fathers, are found to be lacking.

In an effort to further their education, the queen has made plans to send them overseas on diplomatic visits.

With one stroke, Robert Dudley has emptied the court of his rivals. Those who might have spoken out against him with the Duke of Norfolk or Cecil around bite their tongues and looking the other way.

The court, feeling deserted without the presence of the queen's esteemed councillors, grows wilder by the day. The men may sing sonnets and proclaim their undying devotion to Elizabeth, but they sneak into the rooms of others in the evenings to seek their pleasure.

It is during this time that I find myself meeting with Thomas Blount in secret. We take a barge down river and eat supper at an inn. We visit the marketplace and go for a ride in the woods.

But this fairy tale summer must come to an end soon.

"You still say you won't marry me?" Thomas says, his mouth pressing kisses to my neck.

"No," I say, shuddering at his continued caresses. "I've been enjoying this too much to ruin it with the banalities of everyday life."

He nips at my earlobe. "For shame. Think of all the opportunities we would have to spend in each other's arms."

I push him away. "Yes. The one time a year they gave you leave to return home. Look at poor Amy Dudley. She hasn't seen her husband in over a year, and where is he? Playing husband to the queen." I shake my head. "No. If I had to choose, I would play the part of the mistress."

"Don't let your priest hear you say that." Thomas

Blount smiles wistfully.

I get to my feet, pulling the white linen cap back on my head and tucking in the stray strands into place before putting on the French hood. By now, I've become practiced at it.

"You have such lovely hair," he says. "You should always wear it down."

I ignore him. "Is the hood askew?"

He shakes his head and helps me pin it into place.

"I should go. The queen wants my opinion on some fabric."

"Day by day, you grow in her esteem. She will give you a higher position in her household soon," he says.

"I hope that first she will agree to find a place for my son at court. He's nearly eleven now. He could serve as a pageboy."

"I'm sure Sir Robert would take him on. I can have a word with him—"

"And expose us?"

He looks at me incredulously. "Do you think they don't suspect it already?"

I shrug. "What does that matter so long as we aren't open about it? We happen to be lucky we are two old widowers. No one cares what we do, so long as it remains a secret. But if you ask Dudley for this favour, it will be obvious to all. No, Thomas, this is something I must do on my own."

"I know the true reason is because you don't like my master very much."

I get to my feet, shaking out my skirts. "Besides you

and the queen, I feel very few people can put up with him. I'd like him better if he didn't meddle with the queen and toy with her affections."

"What about what we are doing? How is that different?"

"As you've pointed out, we are two nobodies of whom people don't take notice. So let's be happy with that anonymity." I find I can't look him in the eye. "Besides, I do worry for the queen. The longer she stays unmarried, the greater the chances she won't be able to have a child. Who will come after her? Will there be another civil war? Your master interferes with all that. If they were farmers out in Kent somewhere, I would wish them well."

"But since they are not, you wish he would leave court?"

"Yes."

"Then I would be sent away, too. We'd never see each other again."

I smile down at him. "I remember you swearing you'd wait until the end of your days to be with me. You could always leave his service. Has the thought never crossed your mind?"

"Don't ask me to," his face grows withdrawn.

"I wouldn't. I know this is a passing fancy."

He grabs my hand. "It isn't. But I gave Dudley my oath, and I shall serve him until he releases me. Without him, I would never have been in the position I am today. I would never have met you or been able to pay for my son's education."

"I won't mention it again. I don't think I'd like you

half as much as I do if you weren't so loyal."

His smile makes the corners of his eyes crinkle.

Cecil's return to England heralds the end of our carefree summer.

He arrives in the queen's privy chamber expecting a warm welcome but receives a rather cold one instead.

"We have heard of your supposed success," the queen says, shuffling a card deck. Across from her, Dudley is doing his best to look innocent.

"Yes, Your Majesty. France and Scotland both signed the treaty."

"But what of Calais?" she pouts.

"Your Majesty. Truly, we weren't in any position to be making demands. The King of France has agreed to acknowledge you as Queen of England. That in itself was a huge success."

"How so?" she cries, dealing out the cards, all but throwing them on the table. "Was there ever any doubt that I was queen?"

"I can see that you are busy, Your Grace," Cecil says warily, stepping back. "I shall return another time."

"Nonsense." The queen refuses to let him leave. She's in a fighting mood. There's nothing Cecil can do as she continues to berate him for his failings. A smug Dudley watches the proceedings.

"Your majesty, we cannot win back Calais without an army or a marriage alliance."

Dudley mutters something inaudible.

Cecil rounds on him and is too tired to hold back. "Lord Robert, perhaps, you have some misplaced guilt as you failed to defend the city from the French. Your failure should tell you what an impossible task it would be."

He blanches, springing to his feet. "Of what are you accusing me?"

Cecil isn't undaunted by this show of outrage. Perhaps it is cathartic for him to have managed to get a rise out of his rival for the queen's attention.

"Nothing. I'm sure you did your best then, just as I did my best now. There is nothing in my conduct or dealings that would prove the contrary."

Robert laughs. "You think that your pretty speeches and letters will win lasting alliances? Treaties are cemented on the battlefield."

"You should pray they don't. At this moment, England's finances are in dire straits. We don't have the money to fund an army or the number of men required to take on the likes of France or Spain."

Robert Dudley is ready with a retort, but the queen, watching this, interrupts.

"I am tired," the queen says at last. "You may go, Sir William."

"Your majesty." He bows and leaves the room visibly disappointed. This is a project he's been working on for months. Once in Scotland further negotiations took place. It could've fallen apart any moment, but he held it together.

Over the next few days, the queen shows marked favour to poor Cecil, who is still despondent. There are rumours he might retire but, they prove to be false.

As the end of August approaches, the court begins to prepare for the queen's birthday festivities. Dudley is busy planning a brilliant week of celebrations. There will be bearbaitings, a new play, a grand tournament, and endless opportunities to go hunting. The queen languishes on her seat, Kat Ashley fanning her as Dudley goes over what he has planned for each day.

"When shall we sleep?" I ask Catherine Knollys, who hides a smile.

I look down at the piece I am working on. I've used gold thread from the queen's supplies and I'm making good progress at stitching the lion rampant into the cloth. The embroidery will be used for her majesty's frontlet. She is determined that her new gown shall outshine all her others and plans to wear it on her birthday.

The gown is a bronze taffeta, with slashed sleeves revealing the cloth of gold beneath. We will decorate the black satin frontlet with the gold embroidery. Other ladies of her household are busy stitching precious gems into the skirts of the gown. While most of her dresses are worth a fortune, this gown will eclipse them all.

"When do we ever get to sleep?" Catherine Knollys says, nipping off the end of the thread.

Out of the corner of my eye, I catch Lady Katherine

Grey wiping at the corner of her eyes. I motion with my head for Catherine to look towards her.

"What do you make of that?" I ask. "She's been so quiet lately. Hardly like herself at all."

Catherine Knollys nods. "Perhaps it's Jane Seymour. They have taken away the poor girl from court. There are fears she has consumption."

Consumption would be a death sentence.

"I am very sorry to hear that."

September is unseasonably warm this year. On the day of the queen's birthday, she is awakened by the sounds of music drifting up from beneath her window. She emerges from her bedchambers to find her presence chamber decorated with new tapestries and garlands of flowers.

Someone recites a poem dedicated to her while the choir sings her a beautiful song. Robert Dudley has planned everything and is never far from her side.

To the foreign ambassadors watching, this feels more like Dudley is wooing the queen. Strangely, I notice how Cecil clings to the Spanish ambassador's side. The two are always together in deep conversation.

One morning as the queen prepares to go hunting, I give her a gift—a pair of cream gloves lined with ermine and heavily embroidered with motifs of her coat of arms.

"Lady Dorothy," she says, her fingers brushing over the delicate work. "This is finely wrought."

"Thank you, Your Grace," I say with a curtsey.

"All my ladies are so talented. From making delicious tarts, to singing and now to embroidery. You have an eye for it, and the motifs are beautifully arranged."

My cheeks grow hot with the compliment. "It is always a pleasure to work with my needle, Your Grace."

"I shall wear them today," she declares and removes her other gloves in favour of mine.

Dudley leads her out to the courtyard where a new horse is waiting for her. The mare's coat is a dazzling silver. Its striking blue eyes turn to watch the queen approaching. The harness and saddle are a pale cream leather to match the queen's attire.

"You shall be like the goddess Diana riding through the forest," Dudley says to her.

The queen laughs and pets the horse's muzzle gently. "I wish I could be like Diana forever. But I cannot." He looks incredulous. "Have you not heard, Robert? I am being pressured by everyone to marry."

"Then for at least today, you shall be the virgin goddess, come down among us."

Playfully, she swats at him.

A groom comes forward to help the queen mount her horse, but Dudley waves him away. With one fluid motion he lifts the queen with her heavy riding gown into the saddle and bows to her.

As I mount my chestnut gelding, I find Thomas Blount watching me from the crowd. He will not be riding out with the court today. I can tell he longs to be at my side, and I wish I could tell him I feel the same way.

Catherine Knollys pulls her horse up beside me, her

eyebrows raised. "I thought there was nothing to that relationship, but clearly there is."

"Just a bit of playacting."

"Really? At your age?"

I scoff. "I'm in my thirties. Hardly an old crone."

She laughs. "You know I tease you. But I do think you are a bit old for the greensickness of young love."

I pull upon my horse's reins as the baying of the hunting dogs has it pawing the ground. We are all eager to ride out.

"Catherine, I think this is the first time... I've never experienced this sort of passion before. I can understand the queen's difficulties like never before."

"You must take care..." she says, her tone full of warning.

"I know. Don't you think I know? I am so grateful I'm not some great heiress on the marriage mart." My eyes drift over to Katherine Grey. Offers for her hand in marriage have been streaming in, but the queen has been batting them away. Far from minding, Katherine is pleased. Perhaps she has learned to prefer court life as a lady in the queen's train more than one as a wife.

We hunt until well into the afternoon and return just in time for supper.

The queen eats very little and instead calls for dancing to begin.

She leads Dudley out onto the floor. They dance the provocative volta. His hands linger on her person as the music carries them through the steps.

The queen leaps into the air gracefully, as if she is not being encumbered by the heavy gown she wears.

The Spanish ambassador sitting nearby sneers at this indecent display but applauds with the rest of the court as the dance ends.

Dudley leads her back to her seat.

As the queen sits down, he keeps a hold of her hand.

When she looks up at him, to see what he means by holding her hand, he pulls her glove off with one swift flick, exposing her exquisite hand for all to see. From his pocket he draws a brilliant ruby ring and places it on one of her fingers.

She examines the ring and brings it to her lips to kiss it. It's all but a declaration of intent to marry. There is muttering all around the court at this. Cecil shares a pointed look with the Spanish ambassador.

Everyone is so distracted by this that they don't notice the commotion at the back of the hall. I have been trying to spot Thomas, so I'm one of the first to see the messenger trying to push forward.

"My Lord Dudley, I must speak to you," the messenger shouts. There are so many people crowded at the back that he cannot get through.

"Let him come forward," Dudley commands. He straightens, a flash of anxiety in his eyes.

The messenger bows to the queen and then to Dudley, "Sir, I've come straight from Cumnor Place." He chokes on his words. "Your wife was found dead yesterday evening. I've ridden hard, without stopping, to bring you this news. I'm so sorry."

CHAPTER 14

There are gasps of horror all around the great hall. Among all the buzzing, I can hear one thing repeated over and over again: Amy Dudley has been murdered.

"What do you mean she was found dead?" Dudley asks the messenger, but he never hears the answer.

The queen rises from her seat. "I feel unwell. Take me to my room."

Dudley spins around to offer her his arm, but she looks past him as if she cannot see him. Instead, she takes Sir Nicholas Throckmorton's arm.

I get to my feet, as do all her other ladies. There's a scramble as we rush to follow her. No one cares about the order of precedence as we flee to her bedchamber.

By the time we reach the queen's apartments, she is breathing hard, fighting to catch her breath.

"Shall I call the doctor, Your Grace?" Blanche Parry asks.

"No." Elizabeth waves her away. "Thank you, Sir Nicholas. Will you tell Cecil to come to me at once? I must speak to him."

He nods and leaves the queen in our capable hands.

"Undress me," she says, moving about the room. "I can't breathe in this stifling dress."

We rush to do as she bids. The queen's headdress is carefully unpinned, then her sleeves and overcoat are removed. In our rush, items of clothing are strewn about the room.

I step over a hip pad as I whisper to Katherine Grey, "Bring out the green English gown she wore two days ago." Pale-faced, she runs to find it among the queen's trunks.

Now that the queen is stripped down to her linen shift, I hand over a plain green kirtle with a pleated skirt. Over top, Katherine Grey brings out the deep green open gown. Its wide neckline and loose-fitting design will make the queen feel less restricted. We slip it over her shoulders. Her skin is paler than the silver hem. With a look of concern, we close the silver clasps.

After we've finished, she collapses into a chair cradling her head between her hands. Kat Ashley brings her a warm tisane, but she pushes it away.

There's a knock at the door, and Cecil is announced.

The news of Amy Dudley's death might mean the downfall of his greatest enemy, but when he enters the room his face is grim.

"Wait outside," the queen says to us. Only Kat Ashley stays at her side.

My anxiety grows as I wonder what is happening. Not knowing how long Cecil and the queen will be in conference, I slip out of the queen's apartments.

Robert Dudley's apartments are barred, not that I would dare enter but in the hallway I see another of Dudley's men. I stop him with one glance.

"Sir Thomas Blount—where might I find him?"

He looks puzzled by the question but then says, "He's gone, lady. Riding out for Berkshire, on the master's business."

With a mental curse, I turn and head for the stables as fast as I can. He's there packing a saddle bag and soothing the horse.

"What is happening?" I say. "Why must you go to Cumnor Place?"

Thomas doesn't look at me, but his hands go still on the straps of the saddlebags.

"Please," I say pleading. "At least tell me you will return."

He turns. In that moment I am caught by the intensity of his gaze. I desperately need him to kiss me. As if reading my thoughts, he stalks forward. By the time his insistent lips claim my own, I am weak with desire. Together we move, until I am caught between his hard body and the wooden post at my back. We are of one mind as he hikes up my skirts. My hands wrap around his neck.

Anyone could discover us, but we are too far gone in our passion to care. He pulls down my frontlet, exposing my breasts. My breath hitches as he takes one and then the other into his hot mouth. I buck against him, my hands running through his hair as we consummate our relationship in the most unlikely of places. When we pull apart, we are both at a loss for words. His forehead rests against mine as he takes deep steadying breaths.

"I will return, but not before I deal with this matter," he says, placing a kiss on my forehead. "I love you."

"What do you need to do?"

"Amy Dudley has died, but everyone is saying she was murdered. We must discover the truth, and, if someone has murdered her, discover who it is."

I touch his arm. "You don't think it was—Robert Dudley?"

He shakes his head. "Even if the love between them had gone, he would never. She was ill already. There was no reason for him to act."

"Perhaps he grew impatient," I point out.

Thomas shakes his head. "He's too honourable to commit such an atrocity. Besides, he would never risk his chances."

I arch a brow, forcing him to elaborate.

"He would ruin any chances of marrying the queen if he had such a stain on his reputation."

A bitter laugh escapes my lips. "Of course he's been after the crown this whole time. At least you've finally admitted that was his desire."

"Marrying the queen would be the goal of any sane man."

"Even yours?" I say, with a haughty look.

He grins taking up the challenge. "Did I ever say I

was a sane man? I've delayed long enough. I must ride all night. You may not see me for weeks. If they banish my lord from court, know that I love you, and I will wait for you. We'll see each other again."

I nod.

He reaches out, his thumb wiping away the tear sliding down my cheek. Then he is leading his horse out of the stable.

"I love you too," I shout out after him. He turns to wave at me, and then he's off riding into the dark of night.

Wrapping my arms around myself, I stand there trying to process the last few hours. It feels like the world is slipping away from under me.

The next day, the queen is a different creature all together. She has lost none of her vivacity and energy. When anyone mentions Robert Dudley, she says she was sad to hear of his wife's untimely end. The court wears black to honour her as we wait for the investigation and the autopsy to be complete.

Everyone has their own version of events. But at the heart of every tale, Robert Dudley's name appears. Whether he was merely a distant husband who banished his wife from his side or a murderous villain, it seems his reputation will never recover.

When the queen returns from a long walk, she discovers Dudley has sent her a message requesting an audience. In the past, he would have strolled into her rooms without a care in the world. It's telling that he is no longer sure of his welcome.

She passes me the letter, and I cannot help but glance down at the messy scrawl on the parchment.

"Tell your master that it would be impossible at this time to see him. I shall write to him shortly. You can wait here for it," she tells the manservant.

Cecil enters the room just in time to catch her and suggests she doesn't. "It might be best, Your Grace if I were to take your message to him myself."

She frowns, looking ready to protest but then relents. "Very well. Please tell Lord Robert that I am sorry for his loss and I grieve with him. He should retire to his house at Kew to mourn his wife. I know he will want privacy and quiet at a time like this."

We are all astounded, but Cecil, bowing, looks triumphant.

"I shall shortly return, Your Grace."

"Do you think he shall truly be banished from court forever?" I ask Lady Catherine Knollys. Selfishly, all I can think of is Thomas, and I'm sure my features make that evident too.

"I don't see how he can return from this," she says, her features strained by a night spent at the queen's bedside. Neither of them must have got much sleep.

"The queen has always favoured him. Even when all her councillors and her closest confidants urged her to send him away, she refused."

"That was before he murdered his wife."

I wince. "We can't know that."

She looks at me as if seeing me for the first time. "Since when did you become his defender?"

"It's not that," I say, avoiding her avid gaze.

"Oh, I remember now. That servant of his. Are you aching for him?" she whispers. Her tone is teasing, but I'm horrified. I want nothing more than to cover her mouth with my hand to prevent any other incriminating things from escaping.

The court becomes a sombre place as each day passes.

With Dudley out of the way, the foreign dignitaries waiting in the shadows sense an opportunity. Yet until the queen's name is cleared, even their masters are uncertain they would wish to enter marriage negotiations. This turn of events dismays Cecil most of all.

In November, the autopsy confirms that Amy Dudley died from an accidental fall. There are several strange parts in the tale of how this came to be. She had sent her servants out for the day and dined alone in her rooms while they enjoyed a festival. At some point, she must have ventured downstairs when she tripped and fell. But what made her send everyone away? Had she truly been alone? Had someone taken the opportunity to murder her and make it look like an accident?

The official inquest was inconclusive, but it did clear Robert Dudley and the Queen of any obvious wrongdoing.

Dudley is not satisfied with this. He believes he can foresee how the rumours surrounding her death will never disappear until a culprit is found. He pays for another inquest, and witnesses are questioned and cross-examined at great expense to himself. Yet they can find nothing.

The queen orders him to cease this frenzy of investigations and demands he return to London.

Dudley, now a widower, arrives at court hoping things can go back to the way things were. Of course, now that he is an unmarried, it is a very different thing for him to arrive unannounced to the queen's chambers. No longer does she invite him to sit with her alone in her bedchamber to play cards, nor do they disappear into the forest with only a small escort riding behind them.

He grows cantankerous. Meanwhile, the queen is happily setting the boundaries on their new relationship. Seeing that she is in no hurry to marry him, the Holy Roman Emperor once more proposes she marry the archduke.

For the first time, negotiations feel earnest. The queen has Robert Dudley watching from the distance as she laughs and debates with the ambassador about how many sons and daughters she might give to the archduke.

As recompense for the agony, Dudley demands the queen restore him to the peerage.

"After what I have suffered, do I not deserve it?" he says. "I have been the only one there for you from the beginning. Have I not proven my loyalty to you?"

"Robert," the queen sighs. She is exhausted. "You know how I value your friendship. But—"

"Friendship!" he cries out as if she has stuck him. "That stings more than anything else you've said to me."

"Robert," she says warningly. "Don't say something you will regret."

He is red in the face but steps away from her. "I shall return to the country and leave the court. You no longer love me as you once did. It pains me to be with you, yet not with you at all. What has tainted your view of me?"

She gives him a pointed look. Did it need to be said out loud? Whether he was responsible for Amy Dudley's death, he was certainly been the reason the queen's reputation came under question. That was something for which she could never fully forgive him.

We continue our leisurely stroll through the gardens at Greenwich. They were extensively replanted and enlarged last spring, and now in autumn we can enjoy the beautiful pathways and newly installed fountains. I'm dressed in my sombre black, but I have a new brooch pinned to my lapel. It's a pale blue stone cut in the shape of a heart framed by gold vines. Thomas slipped it into my pocket upon his return to court. Unfortunately, he was sent away from court again shortly after arriving.

Up ahead of me, Robert Dudley's voice rises again.

"I'm tired of being looked down upon by the likes of Pickering and even your dear Cecil because I'm reduced to being a beggar. Your sister lifted that attainder against me. Since then, have I not proven my loyalty? It is in your power to grant me my full title back. It is my birthright.

For all the love that you have for me, Elizabeth—" he pauses and corrects himself. "Your Grace. Please consider this small request."

The queen, exhausted from the argument that has been going on for over a week, reaches out to him. "I shall try. Come, let us talk about happier things. You claim you miss me, yet you keep yourself away whenever we have the chance to talk as we once did."

The queen, unwilling to fight or argue with her favourite any longer, announces at a privy council meeting that she wishes to make Robert Dudley an earl.

Predictably, there is outrage and shock.

Later, William Cecil, along with two other members, arrive in her presence chamber to dissuade her.

"Your Majesty, there are other honours you could bestow on him. He is already Master of the Horse and Lord Lieutenant of Windsor Castle. You've given him grants of other land and income on top of this. He is well rewarded already," Cecil says.

I hide a smile at the twinge of jealousy as he lists everything Robert Dudley has been given. This has the opposite effect on the queen, who never enjoys being told what to do.

"It is I who decides who is worthy of being rewarded and how, Sir William. I appreciate your input in this matter, but it is entirely unnecessary." She glances around the room to find the rest of us watching the exchange with rapt attention.

"I must add my own concerns to that of Cecil's, Your Majesty," Lord Henry Carey says. As her cousin, the queen has shown him marked favour. His sister meets his eye, trying to warn him not to proceed, but he either doesn't see or ignores her. "There are already rumours that you merely seek to raise him to the peerage in order to marry him."

Catherine Knollys reaches for my hand for support as we can sense the anger boiling within the queen is about to explode.

"Everything I do, I do for the sake of the realm. Who are either of you to seek to command me? I am the queen! And I will not be led by the nose like some cow to market," she snaps. "Arrange the investiture ceremony. We shall speak no more about this."

"What will the archduke say?" Cecil can't help himself from asking. "We've come so close. He's agreed to your demands regarding religion…"

"That has nothing to do with this. If the archduke seeks to interfere in my realm before we are even married, then I am afraid he is not the husband for me."

Cecil bows his head. He knows there's no point in continuing the discussion now that she has been whipped up into a frenzy.

Even I, who am with the queen day and night, cannot for certainty say what she could be thinking.

"You'll excuse us, Your Majesty," Cecil says, bowing again.

After they leave, the queen deflates. She looks around at us as if she would confide her deepest secrets. Instead she bites her tongue and asks for her needle and thread to be brought to her.

Hours later, she loses patience for needlework and retreats to her rooms. There she spends hours translating the works of Plato from Greek into Latin and then English.

"Your majesty, may I bring you something to eat or drink?" I say, knowing it would be hopeless to ask her to take a break.

She blinks at the sound of my voice. "Drink. Some mulled ale would settle my stomach."

"Of course." I bow.

Moments later, a servant comes running forward with a warmed pitcher of ale. Cardamom and cloves have been added. The drink smells divine.

I bring out two cups. Into one, I pour a mouthful and swish it around in my mouth to taste for anything unusual. Then I place the second cup on her desk, careful not to disturb her papers.

"Ruling over men is a complicated thing," she says to me as she cradles the goblet between her hands. "Even as they swear to adore me and serve me, they seek to undermine my authority."

I don't know if she expects me to reply, so I remain silent, patiently listening.

"In my father's day, his councillors and advisors lived in terror of him. They'd never have dared speak to him as they speak to me. I will remind them I'm the one in command."

"Of course," I say, not sure what she means.

"Show me your latest embroidery work, Lady Dorothy. You truly have a skill for colours and patterns."

CHAPTER 15

S ervants decorate the hammer-beam roof of the great
hall with garlands of roses and hang heraldic banners
on the walls. All the lords and ladies of court and visitors are
invited to witness Dudley's investiture. As I enter, I search
out Thomas Blount in the crowd. He's finally returned to
court, though we have yet to meet in person. Dudley had
named him as the officer in charge of Amy Dudley's funeral
and stayed to discharge the members of her household. I
wait eagerly for the chance to slip away with him. Perhaps
tonight during the banquet will be the perfect opportunity.

They announced the queen with a roll of drums and
a blare of trumpets. She strides into the room in a regal
red gown wearing her robes of state and crown upon her
head.

The Archbishop of Canterbury is there, as is the
Bishop of London, who will read out the letters patent.
Hundreds of other lords and ladies are present. Regard-

less of how they may feel about Dudley, none want to miss the chance to make an appearance at the banquet that will follow.

The queen is a mask of cold serenity as she waits.

The doors are flung open, and Robert Dudley, wearing a suit of fine silver brocade, strides in.

He approaches the queen, kneeling before her on a cushion placed a few feet in front of her.

The Archbishop of Canterbury hands her the letters patent.

She unfurls the parchment, and then to the shock of everyone, pulls a knife from her pocket and slashes the paper in half. We watch in stunned silence as the parchment falls to the floor.

Dudley, red from rage, demands what she means by this.

"I rule here, Lord Robert," she says, her voice carrying around the room for all to hear. "I shall not raise another traitorous Dudley to the House of Lords."

"Why not?" Robert gets to his feet. The Queen's Yeomen of the Guard step forward in case they must intercede. My heart is pounding as I watch this scene unfold.

"I owe you no explanation." The queen dismisses him with a flick of her wrist.

"You promised me. You swore—" He breaks off, remembering where he is. Then, stiffly, he bows and retreats the way he came, his head held high. The doors shut behind him with a resounding thud.

Queen Elizabeth claps her hands together. "Shall we dine?"

We file into the adjoining room, where we remain well into the night. Robert Dudley's enemies feast and celebrate with wild abandon. The wine cups are never empty for long, and there is talk and excited chatter all around the hall. The queen remains composed at the centre of it all. She looks over her courtiers, satisfied they know she is a power to be reckoned with.

It is well after midnight when I catch Thomas Blount sliding into the hall. He waits at the back of the room, but when he sees me watching him, he motions with his head for me to come to him.

Given that most people are too drunk to notice, I leave my table and head out into the corridor beyond.

He comes up behind me minutes later.

With his hand on my elbow, he guides me out into a courtyard nearby.

I want him to embrace me, but he is not in an amorous mood as he looks down at me.

"Did you know she would embarrass him like that?"

"No," I say honestly. "But I had a suspicion she wouldn't go through with it."

He curses under his breath, running a hand through his hair.

"Stop that," I tease. "You'll pull all your hair out."

"Dorothy, can't you see how tormented I am? My master is beside himself."

I shift my gaze away from his face to the gravel at my feet. "You've done all you can do. He overreached himself. You should've seen how he pressed her to make him an earl. He was as relentless as she was cruel."

"They are a perfect match, then," he says to himself.

I grab hold of his hands. "Whether they are does not matter. It should not. Now why are we wasting time when we have so little of it together?"

I move to embrace him, but he steps away. "I must return. He is despondent."

"Don't let his disappointment taint what we have," I say.

"Sometimes you make me forget that duty comes before all else," he says, kissing me.

My lips curl into a smile against his lips. "Funny you should say that. I feel quite the same."

"So you are determined we shall never marry?"

"Yes. But that doesn't mean I don't wish for us to continue seeing each other like this," I say.

"You speak of sin."

"Haven't we already committed it?" I say haughtily. "Given how much we value duty, wouldn't the greater sin be to leave our posts?"

"This is a matter for the priests. Certainly not one we can settle now. I must go, but I will see you as soon as I can," he promises. With one last kiss, he slips away. Once more, I find myself cursing Dudley and his pretensions.

Slowly, the scandal of Dudley's failed investiture dies away, as do the rumours that the queen is going to marry him. Everyone is thrilled, and no one doubts her anymore.

The Christmas season passes, and then there is a fresh scandal for the court to feast on.

In the middle of the night, Thomas appears in the queen's chambers. He finds me awake, ready in case the queen summons me.

"What is it?" I say, since I know he hasn't come just to see me.

He shakes his head dumbfounded. "I cannot say. Sir Robert needs to see the queen immediately."

I raise a brow. "I hardly think she will allow that." As Master of the Horse, Dudley still receives favoured rooms close to the queen's own apartments. He is still allowed to come in and out of her rooms as he pleases, yet a coldness has settled over the pair that may never repair. I doubt she would approve of being pulled out of her bed for this.

"It's urgent," Thomas says. "Cecil too."

Now I can see he isn't joking. "Very well."

Inside, the queen is in her nightgown. She is surprised to find me in her room at all. "Lady Dorothy, what is this?"

"Something has happened. Dudley knows," I say.

"What?"

"He has summoned Cecil to your apartments and will arrive shortly to bring you both the news."

The queen blanches. "Is it the French? Are they invading despite everything?"

I shake my head. "No, I doubt it. He would've said something."

"Send him in the moment he arrives. Tell him he has my permission. And Cecil, where is Cecil?"

"Your Majesty should put on a robe."

The queen looks down at her state of undress as though surprised to find she is no longer in a gown. She snaps her fingers irritated at herself as if she should have foreseen the need to stay in a gown tonight.

I rush over to her wardrobe nearby and pull out a black overcoat. I can only tie it loosely about her and am forced to use a belt to keep it in place. It's the best we can do given the urgency of the situation.

There is a knock at the door, and I open it to find Thomas, Dudley, and Cecil waiting. All three men wear the same stony expression.

"Guard the door, cousin," Robert says to Thomas as they step inside. I shut the door behind them.

The queen, wringing her hands, waits for Dudley to explain himself.

"Lady Katherine Grey has come to me..."

The queen freezes. Given that the queen was worried about a French invasion, I'm surprised by the way she tenses as Dudley stumbles over his words. Has Katherine been smuggled out of England?

"...she says she is with child and that the child was begotten in holy matrimony." Dudley swallows hard.

"Whom?" the queen cries out.

"The Earl of Hertford."

"What?" Cecil says, a combination of shock and relief in his voice.

"Yes. She came to my room this evening and

confessed everything. I sent her away saying I could not help her. Then, I came straight to you," Dudley says to Elizabeth. "I had no idea."

"Why would she come to you?" she hisses.

"She thought I would be sympathetic to her cause. Or maybe that I would help persuade you not to be angry."

The queen scoffs. "She knows that as a member of the royal family, she is forbidden to marry without my permission. Katherine Grey is nothing but a traitor to the crown."

"Your Majesty," Cecil interrupts. "You've never acknowledged that. You cannot be surprised that she might see matters differently." He glances at me as if for help. "I warned you to be kinder to her and make it clear to parliament about your wishes regarding her status."

"That changes nothing. According to the Act of Succession, she is in line for the throne and thus cannot marry on a whim. It is a sham. It must be." The queen rounds on Dudley. "And you say she is with child?"

He nods, then adds, "I am not a physician or midwife, but I doubt she would lie about such a grave matter."

"What a brilliant play on her part," the queen says to herself. "And you, Cecil, what do you say about all of this?"

"Summon the Earl of Hertford back home. We will investigate and get to the bottom of this."

"I want her arrested," the queen snaps.

Cecil hesitates. "I don't know —"

"Arrested. Kept under lock and key and questioned."

"She is a member of the royal family, as you claim. Do you think that is wise?"

"Then give her the most luxurious rooms you can think of. But I want her out of my sight."

"We could put her under house arrest," Cecil offers.

"No, that would not be enough. She could find a way to escape. Who knows what else she is plotting?"

Robert and Cecil look at each other, knowing it is hopeless to argue with the queen now that she's worked herself into a state of anxiety.

"Very well, Your Majesty. You must remember that your cousin is young and foolish," Cecil says. "This is likely nothing more than two young people marrying for love but, we will leave no stone unturned."

"Cecil," the queen says, her voice steady. "She will be kept in the Tower. Spare no expense on her comfort, but I will not have her roaming free. The Catholics would love to rally behind a married Catholic heir who—if—" Elizabeth puts a hand to her mouth. "If she has a legitimate son, she will become my greatest rival."

Cecil stares at the carpet. "Yes. I pray to God that you will see how precarious your situation is now. The longer you remain unmarried, the greater the risk to yourself and the realm."

The queen ignores him. "She cannot bear a legitimate son." She fixes Dudley with a knowing look. "As you have said, Sir William, she is a foolish young lady. I doubt she and the earl are properly married. It's far more likely he tricked her, or they merely made empty promises." She starts listing off any number of possibilities.

I stare at my hands as the queen sets about planning how to tear apart a young woman's life. Katherine Grey has never been a friend. But hearing the queen now, I know she will spend at least a few months behind bars until the matter is cleared up. When she emerges, her reputation will be in shatters. I fear for her and her unborn child. For the first time in my life, I am glad that my family has fallen into obscurity.

Once the queen is in bed, I leave her bedchamber and make my way out into the corridor, past the guards stationed at the doors. There is nothing particularly suspicious about a lady-in-waiting leaving at night. They've seen both Cecil and Dudley go in and are more likely to assume I'm on another errand for the queen.

I find Thomas Blount waiting for me outside of Dudley's rooms. Taking his arm, we walk hand in hand to a private chamber where I let him know what has transpired in a hushed whisper.

He holds my hand in his. As I continue my tale, he traces circles on my palm.

"And here I thought to entrap you into marriage," he said.

I shake my head, unable to find the serenity to joke with him. "It won't matter if Lady Katherine Grey was married by the archbishop himself. The queen will fabricate some reason that the marriage is not valid at all to ensure her child won't have a valid claim to the throne. It will have the added benefit of ruining Katherine's reputation."

"It wouldn't be the same for us. And we could proceed through the proper channels," Thomas says.

"This has to be enough," I say.

"It is," he reassures me even as I hear the doubt in his voice.

I lean against him for support. "You know, while legally dubious, it is enough for us to hold our hands fast together and swear an oath in order to be married in the eyes of God."

"I believe witnesses are required."

"God is everywhere, is he not?" I point out. Had we not debated this very matter of theology today at court? "He is our witness."

He grins. "We should at least say our oaths in a chapel."

"If that's what it would take to please you."

He kneels before me, kissing my hands. "I adore you, Dorothy. Marry me on a date of your choosing. I swear to always honour you and think of you as my true wife."

"And no one else can know."

"Your wish is my command."

Two days later, we contrive a reason to meet in the queen's chapel while everyone else is at supper. Before the bare altar, we say our vows and seal them with a chaste kiss. For better or worse, our fates are entwined.

CHAPTER 16

1563-1564

"You've added too much egg white." I scold the new maid-in-waiting as she mixes the queen's face lotion. "The measurements need to be exact."

"I'm sorry," the young girl says.

Taking a deep breath, I push aside my annoyance, remembering that next year my daughter will join the queen's service. I hope that whoever is teaching her will be patient.

"Just make sure to add more alum."

Then we move on to making the white paste that will be painted on to her majesty's skin. Once she finishes, I test it on the back of my hand before adding a dash more vinegar.

"See," I show the girl. "This is the consistency we need so that it spreads easily yet covers the skin. There's also a brilliant sheen to it when the light hits it just right."

Eager, the maid-in-waiting nods.

I hand the two jars to Catherine Knollys, who is

waiting nearby. The lotion will be applied to the queen's face, neck, and hands, ensuring every inch of exposed skin will be covered by the white cosmetic paste we have made. Once applied, we will pretend the queen has achieved the perfect complexion she once possessed.

It's hard to think that a year ago we came so close to losing her. Smallpox is a deadly disease, and there were many times when we thought she'd die. The queen made her will, though she stopped short of naming her successor. Then to everyone's relief, she began to recover. Only the pockmarks—faint as they are—remain. They serve as a warning of crisis that could have been and will surely come in the future because the queen still has no heir.

She has not married, nor named a candidate. If anything, she has removed a few names from the line of succession.

Poor Katherine Grey is under house arrest in Suffolk. She endured a long imprisonment in the Tower of London after they declared her marriage invalid and her two sons became bastards. It's terrible to imagine that for the rest of her life they will keep her separated from her children and would-be husband. Katherine is absolutely alone, away from the things that always brought her joy. I can only think of her with pity.

Thomas and I see each other whenever we can. Even after all these years, Robert Dudley is still the queen's favourite. Recently, she gave him Kenilworth Castle. He swore he would have her visit him on one of her progresses. But as far as Thomas can see, it will take a lot of work and money to fix the castle and improve it to the queen's exacting standards.

Cecil has stopped pressing the queen to marry. In an act of desperation, he even insisted that he would support her marrying Dudley. But the queen is content to keep delaying.

When she called her parliament and asked them to grant her more funds, they agreed to do it on the condition she settle the matter of succession once and for all.

Her response: a flat no. She deferred and made endless excuses. Then, after a moving speech, assured them that when God would present her with a worthy husband, she would marry.

Impressed by her passion, they agreed to give her the money she requested. Only later did they realise that, in fact, she had agreed to nothing concrete.

I admire the queen far more than I ever thought possible. Against all odds and even the expectations of her councillors, Elizabeth defies all expectations, proving that women are capable of governing.

"How does your son, Edward, like the court?" the queen says to me as they fix her hair into place.

"He's honoured to be here, Your Grace."

At the moment, he is working with Throckmorton in the Chamber of the Exchequer. From what he told me, most of his days are spent digging out obscure bills and helping to file the constant paperwork coming in. The queen employs a small army of clerics to manage and keep track of her finances. When she can, she prefers to be frugal.

I have begun to suspect she prefers this penny-pinching to asking parliament for more money. Who knows what demands they might in exchange for the funds?

"I'm more than happy to employ smart young men at my court. I can't do everything on my own," she says.

With the queen dressed, she emerges out into her privy chamber, where Cecil and Robert Dudley await. They are planning her summer progress, and she has expressed the wish to visit the universities. Elizabeth has been studious her whole life. Her love of learning has never ceased, and even now she is eager to find people with whom to debate and discuss various topics. Her pride in her intelligence is well known, and she would never shrink from the opportunity to show it off.

"There is Cambridge, Your Majesty," Cecil says. "You have yet to pay a visit to it."

"Yes, spirit. I would enjoy the chance to inspect all the work you have done as Chancellor. By all accounts, it's thriving."

He nods but adds, "I hope you will think so."

"There is something else I wish to discuss," the queen says, moving around the table to look at the drawn map of England. "Sir Francis Walsingham confirms that Queen Mary has decided against a Spanish alliance. Perhaps now is our chance to put forward our own suitor."

Cecil glances at Dudley who is doing his best to avoid looking at the queen all together.

"We could revive that possibility," Cecil says, tentatively. "There isn't much chance of success."

"Why ever not?" Elizabeth looks at her favourite with the critical eye of a horse breeder. "He's handsome, tall and strong. What could she possibly not like about him?"

I would bet that Cecil is thinking just what I am thinking. Perhaps the queen of Scotland would not appreciate having her cousin's lover as a husband. Whether or not it's true.

"There is the matter of my lack of fortune or status," Dudley says at last. "I have nothing I could offer the Queen of Scotland."

The queen waves away his concerns. "She'd be winning my favour by marrying you and cementing a strong alliance with England."

Dudley pulls her away towards an oriel window.

As discreetly as possible, I follow them.

"You really mean to send me away?" he asks in a hushed whisper.

"For the good of the realm, we must all make sacrifices." The queen sniffs.

"If that is what you wish. Then I am yours to command."

"I should hope so, my sweet robin." She places a hand on his forearm then pulls away. Returning to Cecil, she says, "It's settled. Arrange an audience with the Scottish ambassador."

The queen meets with the ambassador in her private garden. The roses are in full bloom and fill the air with their fragrant scent. It's the perfect backdrop for a conversation about marriage.

The Scots ambassador arrives with a gift of a diamond pendant for the queen. She thanks him profusely, and I come forward to pin it to her headdress. Taking his arm, they wander around the garden, first discussing his stay in London, the weather, and many other banalities. Finally, the conversation turns to the Scottish queen.

"We were grieved to hear that my cousin has not found a suitable match," the queen says. "I have written to her on more than one occasion she should come to me for help in this matter."

He bows his head in acknowledgement. Walking behind them, I can see how his shoulders tense. The muscles at the back of his neck look strained.

"Your majesty will recall that my queen would be happy to allow you to choose her husband on the condition your formally acknowledge her as your heir."

Rather than be angry, the queen chuckles. "I wish it were that simple, Sir James. You don't know the trouble it would cause if I were to do that. However, you can reassure her that if she marries someone I pick, she would certainly be my first choice to wear the crown of England after I am gone."

He looks to his left, pretending to admire the roses to hide his annoyance.

"And whom would Your Majesty suggest?"

The queen's lyrical laughter fills the air. "Oh, I could not say. But assure your mistress that he is a fine gentleman, and she will find no reason to complain about him."

"Your majesty, I must know his name."

They continue on in this manner for quite some time. They move inside to her privy chamber, where the queen invites him to see her private collection of portraits and miniatures.

"It's Robert Dudley of whom I speak."

I catch the way the ambassador's hand twitches as if he is fighting the urge to clench his hands into fists.

"Ah. Are you sure you could part with such a loyal and close friend, Your Majesty?"

"Of course."

She goes on to discuss his many favourable traits.

"Perhaps you'd wish to marry him yourself, then."

She shakes her head. "Alas, no. I prefer my unmarried state."

The ambassador's eyes crinkle in amusement.

"My cousin seems less inclined to remain unmarried than I am. Otherwise, I would encourage her to remain so." She clears her throat. "I am planning on having Dudley invested as Earl of Leicester. That would raise him to the peerage and might make my cousin look upon him as a better prospect, would it not?"

"It certainly would," Sir James Melville says but without conviction.

After the interview draws to a close, I slip out to meet with Thomas in secret and tell him all that I heard.

"Sir Robert has been hoping for this for quite some time. The queen mentioned it to him, but he dared not believe that he would finally become a peer once more," he says, drawing me close.

"If he leaves for Scotland, you must not go," I say, my mind already jumping far into the future.

"I will try to stay in England. He relies on me more and more to manage his estates, so I can foresee him making me the caretaker of his lands here if he were to go."

I let out a sigh of relief.

"Don't fret. Who knows what the future holds for us?"

While the two queens send out letters and assurances to each other of their continued love and friendship, the summer season takes Queen Elizabeth out of the city and on progress.

I find it gruelling to always be on the road, travelling from one house to another. More often than not, I am sharing a bed with a generous Catherine Knollys.

The queen's first stop is at Cambridge, where Cecil, learning a thing or two from Robert, has prepared a magnificent celebration.

On the day we are to set out, I send out her black riding gown and match it with a dusty rose kirtle and petticoat. The effect is striking and brings out the colour in her cheeks. For her headdress, I select a beautiful velvet cap bejewelled with pearls and other gems. She glances at herself in the looking mirror and then back at me.

"This is beautifully put together," she says. "I look like a regal scholar."

"You will certainly outshine everyone."

She turns in the mirror. "I've noticed your knack for clothing and haven't forgotten your exquisite needlework."

"You honour me, Your Grace," I say, keeping my head lowered demurely.

"No," she says. "You see, that is the problem. I haven't properly rewarded you for your services to me. But I promise I shall."

My cheeks flush with excitement. She's already assisted me so much by finding places for my older children in her household. Over the years, I've slowly amassed some savings that will go to educating my children and dowries for the girls when they are to be married. Now I am honoured merely to serve her.

As expected, the queen dazzles the waiting crowd with her finery. Yet, it is the way she greets them with heartfelt thanks that wins their hearts. No one is too lowly for her attention. She takes the offered presents directly before passing them to a page to tuck away for later.

Cecil leads the tour around the university. At various stops, she hears debates, speeches, and even a play put on by the students.

Our stay is prolonged and would go on longer if there was enough food and drink for the court.

When the court goes out for a ride, I stay back to oversee the packing of the queen's garments and account for all the jewels. I make a note of anything that is missing, even if it is just a silver pin. It's common for things to disappear whether it's in someone's pocket or simply stuck between the floorboards.

Thomas Blount, making some excuse, appears in the queen's chambers. Once I am done, I find him waiting nearby.

"I thought we could take a stroll," he says. "You haven't been to see the chapel, have you? The queen was rather taken by it."

"Will we have time?" I look towards the road in the direction the queen rode.

He tucks my hand in the crook of his arm. "They won't notice us, even if they are back before we are."

As we walk, we discuss our plans over the upcoming days. He tells me he will travel to Kenilworth Castle before Christmas to oversee the installation of the new roof on the gatehouse.

Coming up the path, we arrive at the chapel. One of the two large wooden doors is propped open. Thomas urges me to go first. Entering the chapel is to step into another world. The cream-coloured stone and light filtering in through the stained-glass windows instantly puts me at ease. At first, I don't even know where to look.

With a smile at my stunned expression, Thomas leads me down the centre of the empty pews towards the rood screen.

"Look up," he says.

I have to blink at the stunning sight. The vaulted ceiling with its intricate stonework pattern is dizzying.

"One of the highest in the world," he tells me, his hands resting on my shoulders.

With mute astonishment, I continue to wander around the chapel admiring the various stained-glass windows. Beneath, the stone walls are carved with heraldic symbols—the Tudor rose being the most prominent.

"Work on the chapel was only completed during the queen's grandfather's reign," Thomas says. "A true marvel of architecture."

I nod. "It's so tranquil."

"Just wait until you hear Mass here tomorrow. The choir will fill the chapel with song. It will be as if the angels have come among us."

"Thank you for bringing me here," I say, resting my head against his shoulder when I hear approaching foot-steps. I move away from him so when the priest comes upon us, he merely sees us examining the stained-glass window of the marriage of Joseph and Mary.

"May I help you?" he inquires politely.

"We've come to admire your beautiful chapel. I hear tomorrow the queen will be invited to hear the choir sing. Is that correct?"

He nods, taking in my fine gown and jewels.

"Where will she be sitting?"

The priest clears his throat. "We have arranged a special seat for her majesty just over there. She will be closest to the rood screen."

I consider the space and the light. Tomorrow, she was going to wear a gold overcoat with a long train of golden gauze, but now I feel that would make her melt into the background. The ruby red or emerald green gown would suit her better.

"Thank you." I incline my head. "Can you escort me back, Sir?" I ask Thomas. For the benefit of the priest, I speak to him with formality.

We retreat the way we came and are back in the queen's apartments before the rest of the court arrives. The following day, the queen, as ever, stuns the gathered scholars in a velvet green gown with cloth of gold sleeves.

Throughout the rest of the summer's progress, the queen turns more and more to me for advice on her wardrobe. When we return to London, she calls me for a private audience and informs me she wishes to name me Mistress of the Robes.

I fall to my knees before her. "I am not worthy of such an honour," I say. Indeed, being named Mistress of the Robes would make me one of the most powerful women at court with direct access to the queen's clothing and jewels. I could draw upon the exchequer for funds to replenish her wardrobe and assign the ladies of the bedchamber their duties. During official state functions, I would help organise and be front and centre among her ladies. No longer would I be shoved to the back of the crowd. On the other hand, I'd never enjoy anonymity. Would it go unnoticed if I disappeared for an afternoon to eat at a tavern with Thomas? Not likely.

"Are you saying I am mistaken in my judgment?" The queen grins down at me.

"No, Your Majesty."

"Good. Then rise."

My heart is pounding as the queen smiles at me and asks me to send for Dudley.

CHAPTER 17

1564

"Sir James Melville will be at the forefront during the ceremony," Cecil says as we go over Dudley's investiture. It is part of my duty as Mistress of the Robes to assist in the planning of all state affairs.

"I've ordered a dozen carpets to be brought out of storage for the occasion. The queen will be in her formal robes of state, and I am told Robert Dudley will be dressed in a silver suit. He should be informed to avoid wearing red or silver."

"I shall make a note of it," Cecil agrees. Everything is a performance, and this ceremony is no exception. The queen, above all, must shine and exemplify the regal glory of her station.

"And the Hapsburg envoy? Shall he also be given a place of honour? Perhaps, the queen could be gracious enough to send him a new suit for the occasion. I believe he prefers navy blue."

Cecil's lips purse into a thin fine line. "Yes. It would

be a gesture of goodwill towards him. He will return home soon."

"I am sorry nothing has come of that," I say. We skirt around the topic of the queen's continued refusal to marry. Most recently, she has once again refused the archduke. The emperor, with his injured pride over her first refusal, had hesitated to make another formal proposal. I can only imagine how hard Cecil worked to convince him to renew the marriage negotiations. What assurances had he made only for them to fall apart now?

"Perhaps next year," Cecil says, yet there's no conviction behind the sentiment.

I've taken to my duties with all the solemnity and gravitas that the position requires. It's hard to fend off all the attention that my new status has given me. Besides the queen, I've become one of the most popular ladies at court.

Catherine Knollys, entering my new room, sighs enviously. "I knew that one day you would eclipse me."

I feel a swell of pride, but I rush to reassure her. "The queen still holds you in high favour. You are the principal lady of her bedchamber."

"Yes," she acknowledges. "Though I don't possess the skills you do. You have a head for managing everything, whereas I fumble my way over accounts and figures. But I am here to celebrate with you, not wallow in self-pity."

She hands me a tankard of wine. "My husband swears it's the best we've produced so far."

We say a toast to the queen and drink heartily while I offer her a plate of mincemeat pies.

"Have you completed all the arrangements for Edward to study at Pembroke College?" Catherine asks.

I nod. "His grandfather doesn't approve, but the knowledge will be useful to him. Who knows? One day, if he serves the queen well, she might make him a lord, with lands and an estate of his own." I could laugh. Where once that had been a mere dream, now it may very well be a possibility. At the very least, I could win him a knighthood.

"And your other children? Have you made grand plans for them?"

I grin. "When would I have had the time?"

"Ha."

With a far-off look, I say, "I intend for John to enter the church. But it is too soon to tell if he will be suited for the task. It was his godfather's greatest wish." Wistfully, I think of the years spent in Geneva. It feels so long ago now. Earlier this year, when news reached England that John Calvin died, I felt the loss deeply. Not only was he a brilliant scholar and theologian, but on a personal level, he assisted my family so much. I am filled with regret that I never got the chance to thank him properly.

On the day of Dudley's investiture, St. James Place is abuzz with activity. As I rush around ensuring clothing and jewellery are delivered from the royal wardrobe into the hands of the proper recipients, I run into Thomas.

"I've come from Sir Robert," he says with a weary smile. "He sends me to ask if there might be some silver buckles he can borrow."

"Ah, I think I have a box right here. Come look at them and pick out the most suitable," I say, motioning him over. I remove the set of keys that hangs on my girdle and search for the correct one. The queen's treasures are kept locked away and I am one of the few honoured with the keys to access them.

Thomas takes his time considering the options.

"I've missed you," he whispers, his thumb skimming over the back of my hand.

My eyes flutter closed for a moment, my body aching for more of his touch. "I know. But I cannot. At least not now. We will have to make do."

"I did not mean it as a reproach. I'm happy to have got the chance to see you for even this moment."

I tilt my head. "You might offer him these," I say, holding up a silver button embossed with the Tudor emblem.

Thomas nods. "They are perfect." Then, leaning closer, whispers in my ear, "As are you."

I fight back a smile and nudge him away gently with my elbow. "Be gone with you or your master will be late," I tease.

The presence chamber, one of the grandest in the

kingdom, is filled with the most illustrious people in the land. All have come to witness this event. Many have come to see if the queen will go through with it this time. Others are looking for a chance to catch the queen's attention and, perhaps, supplant the old favourite. Many are here to place bets on whether Dudley will become the future King of Scotland.

I am already feeling exhausted.

There have been festivities all week, from jousts to feasts. Earlier in the day, there was a banquet. Another is to follow. How I'm to remain on my feet throughout the day is beyond me, but somehow I must.

In the end, the ceremony in which Robert Dudley becomes Earl of Leicester eclipses all other events this year. It's touching to see the pride in his eyes as the archbishop reads out his new titles.

In the days that follow, Melville prepares to return home to Scotland. The queen believes there is a real chance Queen Mary will consider Robert Dudley as a husband. Cecil writes out a list of assurances should Queen Mary agree.

Thomas is the one who tells me that Melville told Dudley in private he is unworthy of the Scottish crown. I don't know whether I should report this to Queen Elizabeth. At the moment, she and Queen Mary are the best of friends, exchanging letters with each other and hoping to arrange a meeting. She might not take the news well.

Instead, I go to Cecil. He seems unsurprised by this. If anything, he looks pleased, as if everything is falling into place.

"Have you heard anything about Lord Darnley?" he asks.

"Not that I know of. The Scots lord certainly did not look his way once during the ceremony or the banquet that followed."

"Interesting." Cecil rests a hand on his desk. "One would think Darnley would take this opportunity to plead the case for the restoration of his lands in Scotland. His mother has been pressing the queen to help her for years. If I were to guess, either Darnley is a fool, or he has already spoken to Melville in secret."

"Why couldn't he be both?" I say getting to my feet, ready to leave. It is not for me to comment on the comings and goings of the likes of Lord Darnley. The young man is a Katherine Grey reincarnate. Through his mother, he has a claim to the English throne and, like Katherine, is as foolish as they come. The queen may have given him preference and a position at her court, but he is the sort of young man who squanders the opportunity in favour of gambling and drinking the days away.

Cecil's broad smile tells me he agrees with me.

"She's insufferable," the queen says to us in a fresh burst of fury. We'd been working hard on stitching shirts for the poor while she reads her correspondence. I put down my needle, knowing it would be futile to continue.

"Who, Your Majesty?" Lady Mary asks.

"My cousin, the Scots queen, thinks she can make demands of me. Am I not a monarch in my own right? I am not a beggar at her doorstep."

The queen continues speaking in general terms, refusing to discuss the details of her letters. But most of us know by now that she is furious over Queen Mary's refusal to marry Robert Dudley. A Scottish messenger brought a long list of demands from Mary before she would even consider entering formal marriage negotiations. Demands, the Queen of Scots must know, will never be met.

"Is there some fresh development?" I ask, calmly enough. It does little to stop Queen Elizabeth's mounting anger.

"She all but commands me to allow Darnley to visit her in Scotland. He is my subject, not hers."

I hum in agreement.

"She doesn't know what an empty-headed fool he is. I know she is thinking of him as a potential match."

"Why not allow him to go, then?"

She fixes me with one of those piercing looks. I hurry to add, "The worst that could happen is they marry, and Queen Mary finds herself saddled with a most unsuitable husband."

The queen chuckles at that. "Then she will rue the day she refused my Robert." She clicks her tongue on the roof of her mouth in displeasure. "But I don't think I shall let him go. If she wishes to marry him, she must approach me. We can forge an alliance between our two nations, but first I will show her she cannot command me."

The queen, urged by Cecil and Dudley working in tandem, agrees to allow Darnley to visit Scotland. They say it will tempt the Queen of Scots into being agreeable to a match with Robert.

Unfortunately, the minute Darnley leaves England, he forgets all about his promises and oaths to Queen Elizabeth. Once he made his petition in Scotland, he was to have returned home to England. Instead, he kneels at Queen Mary's feet, and she makes him her sword bearer. News of their impending marriage reaches England, and though Queen Elizabeth makes a show of her displeasure, there is no real rage behind her threats. We can all see how pleased she is by the news.

She may have lost the chance to negotiate her cousin's marriage, but, ultimately, her goal was achieved. Queen Mary, rather than making a dangerous marriage with a foreign power, is marrying a nobody. Four years later when Mary, Queen of Scotland, forced to abdicate her throne and flees to England, she will discover that Queen Elizabeth will recall every insult.

In the dead of night, the Queen Elizabeth's councillors gather in her privy chambers to discuss what they should do with the Queen of Scots.

I am among the few of her ladies allowed into the

room. What should be an honour is feeling like an ordeal.

"We cannot ignore that there are those in the North who view Queen Mary as the rightful heir to the English throne with a better claim to it than yourself, Your Grace," the Duke of Norfolk says.

The queen pacing in front of the warm fire, spins on her heel and snaps at him. "Isn't the North under your jurisdiction? Are you saying you are harbouring traitors?"

He pales but doesn't back down. "No, of course not. But what is in the hearts of men is not so easily determined."

"She's never been your friend. I don't wish to name her as a rival, but that is what she aspires to be. You cannot forget how she covets your throne," Robert Dudley says. "She has powerful friends overseas who'd be happy to use her as a figurehead to see you overthrown."

There are murmurs of agreement around the table.

The queen scoffs but cannot argue. The archbishop opens his mouth to say something but William Cecil, whose been quiet this entire time, clears his throat.

All eyes turn to him.

"It is becoming increasingly clear to me we must focus on dismantling her support network. The most effective way to do this is to ruin her reputation," Cecil begins. "She calls you a heretic, Your Grace, and we know she writes to the Pope to have you excommunicated. By Catholics near and far, she is seen as their saviour. A godly queen who has done her duty and provided her realm with two sons to inherit her kingdom. It's no wonder many Catholics—" he pauses, seeing the queen's darkening expression. Even a powerful man like him cowers under her displeasure. "—mistakenly wish for her to take your throne. Whether or not we return her to Scotland, we must ensure her reputation is destroyed so no one will support her claim. Fabricated as it is."

"At the very least, her allies will abandon her," the queen finishes out loud.

Cecil inclines his head in agreement.

"Darnley's assassination." The queen stops her pacing and comes forward to address her advisors. "That is the excuse we will use." She turns to Sir Francis Knollys. "You will take charge of her. Ride to greet her and welcome her on my behalf."

Walsingham chimes in, "she will have crossed the border in haste. I doubt she would have anything with her."

The queen nods, "Sir Francis will ensure she is provided with everything she could need. She will see how charitable the English are. But you must make sure she stays put. Mary cannot be allowed to come and go as she pleases."

"Then it is settled. We will wait and see how this plays out," Cecil says.

"And in the meantime, we will not waste time. We must gather evidence and prepare our case," the queen says, looking to her spymaster. His expression is grave as he agrees. I am certain he already has plenty of evidence against Mary—real or not.

The queen continues, "Lord Thomas, you will head in inquiry into her conduct. We will do properly this in the eyes of the law. We may not charge her, of course, but the trial alone should be enough to cast doubt on her character."

Norfolk is pleased by the trust she's placed in him. I wonder how long it'll take him to realise that once again the queen has sent him far from court.

With their business concluded, they all rise and bowing retreat from the room one by one.

Catherine Knollys squeezes my hand tightly before following her husband. I cannot help but feel sorry for her. They will once again face the pain of separation as their duty keeps them apart.

"I am at a loss for what to do," she says to me. "She is a fellow monarch. The Scottish lords simply cannot be allowed to get away with such grievous insults to her person. On the other hand, she is my greatest rival."

I nod, watching the seamstress take the queen's measurements for a new gown.

"You are in a difficult position."

"And no one, not even you, is of any help." She fusses with the mock-up of the sleeves.

"God placed you on the throne to help lead us."

Her eyes flash with challenge. "And did He not also place you here to advise me? The cares of the world cannot be placed on my shoulders alone."

I bow my head. "You are correct. But truthfully, I don't think anyone has ever been put in the situation you are in."

The queen is silent for a moment, then says, "I shall have to navigate this treacherous terrain somehow. Once we are finished here, send someone for Cecil."

"Yes, Your Majesty."

I find it difficult to understand why the queen would go through such lengths to help Queen Mary when she has been such a thorn in her side for years. Her marriage to Darnley might have been a failure but it united both their claims to the English throne. This was further cemented by the birth of their two sons. During their short marriage, Mary continuously sought the assistance of other Catholic powers in Europe to help her overthrow Elizabeth. Letters are intercepted to several Catholic English lords calling on them to rise against their anointed queen. If I were Elizabeth, I wouldn't hesitate to send such a dangerous cousin away. I certainly wouldn't consider helping her.

When the Duke of Norfolk concludes his inquiry the shocking revelations of the casket letters puts an end to all talks of forcing the Scottish lords to take her back as their queen. The letters are proof that she knew of her husband's assassination. Many doubt their authenticity but it doesn't stop Mary's allies from distancing themselves from her.

In the end, Queen Elizabeth decides her cousin is to remain in England, as her honoured guest. She chooses Catherine Knollys' husband to run her household.

However, she is not free to leave the house, receive letters or visitors without the queen's express consent. While she doesn't say it, Elizabeth has essentially imprisoned her cousin.

"I wish he would not go so far from me," Catherine says, dabbing her face with a kerchief to dry her tears. "I've been feeling unwell."

"Hush, now," I say, taking her hand in mine. "Once this cold has abated, you will feel better. It's so damp these days that even I find myself coughing a lot. I'm certain that this business with Queen Mary will be over soon and he will return to court."

I am wrong. The Scottish queen is not returned to her throne. Her arrival in England heralds a tumultuous time for us all. Furious at what she sees as Elizabeth's betrayal, she swears she will take her throne from her. It's not an empty threat either. Even kept under house arrest, her religion, birth, and natural vivacity are enough to spark the flame of rebellion in the English subjects.

The queen discovers that even the ties of blood and kinship are not enough to keep those like the Duke of Norfolk loyal to her. She forgives him once, accepting his excuses, but after Cecil and Walsingham uncover a second attempt to free Queen Mary, Elizabeth takes the duke's head. It serves as a warning to all those who thought her weak and too kind-hearted to do what is necessary to survive.

As always, the queen's intelligence and political savvy go underestimated.

Had she been quick to punish him, the common

people would have pitied the duke and she would've risked sparking further uprisings in her nation.

There are times when I find myself at my wit's end, yet never once do I yearn to be an obscure country lady. The one thing I do regret is that Thomas and I must continue to keep our relationship secret. We have an understanding of each other that goes deeper than the need to declare to the world I am his and he is mine. In our hearts we know our love burns true. Perhaps, that is why we are such a perfect pair.

EPILOGUE

Harp music fills the air as the queen's great procession arrives at Kenilworth. As I ride behind the queen, I wonder how long the musicians have been perched up in the trees waiting for our arrival. We were delayed for several hours when we stopped to dine with Robert Dudley, the Earl of Leicester a few miles up the road.

I try to take in every little detail as we approach the brightly lit house for it represents the culmination of a decade of work for Thomas.

The castle, rather than being torn down and rebuilt as a modern palace, has been repaired and expanded. It looks like a mighty fortress rather than a gentleman's country estate.

The queen is quite taken by it.

Clearly, the earl has spared no expense to entertain her. It becomes abundantly clear to me the longer the visit continues he is trying to woo her in earnest. In her forties, the queen doesn't have time to waste. By this point no one would complain if she were to marry Dudley so long as she gave England an heir. I pity the pressure placed on her. She has already sacrificed so much to serve the realm tirelessly for all these years. Is it not enough?

Amidst the celebrations and hunts in the deer park nearby, I meet with Thomas.

He takes me out of Kenilworth through the back stairs and secret passageways until we emerge at the stables. There we mount horses, and he leads me to a small hunting lodge deep in the woods. It is still under construction, and he assures me there's no risk of any visitors.

We languish together on plump cushions for the entire morning while we feast on hard cheese and wine.

"Did you plan this all yourself?" I tease him. "Or did you order some servant to carry this all here?"

"It was all me." He leans forward, tapping my nose. "I'm sure I got strange looks smuggling out pillow after pillow."

I grin as I stretch myself out. "It was worth every effort you made. I hope it proved worthwhile for you, my love."

He caresses my bare hands. I note they are no longer the hands of a young woman. They are veined and marked by time, yet the adoration he shines upon them— upon me—reassures me I am cherished.

"Shall we end our days like the lovers in one of those

tragic plays you enjoy watching?" His hand is trailing down my back.

"Nay," I say, sitting up. "And I shall tell you why. Rather than the passionate romances that end in death, I want a quiet, steadfast love that endures for years to come. I want us to grow old and senile together."

He laughs. "Perhaps, by then, we will be asked to retire from our duties. Then we will be forced to spend the rest of our days together in a small cottage just like this one."

I smile, resting my head on his chest. His arms envelop me in a tight embrace.

"Perhaps. You know, I never imagined I would travel the world and serve the Queen of England. I have distinct memories of being young and desperate to escape a small provincial life. My dreams were so grand. But after all this time, it wouldn't be so wrong to dream of a future spent in your arms, would it?"

He chuckles against my greying hair. "You always want the best of everything. I pray life never disappoints you."

"It won't, because I won't let it."

AUTHOR'S NOTE

Lady Dorothy Stafford outlived the queen by a year. She lived to be seventy-eight, a rarity in those times. For over forty years, she faithfully served the Queen in several capacities. Her children achieved respectable places in society, thanks in large part to the connections she made.

As far as the records go, Dorothy never remarried. However, in this novel, I suggest she entered into some sort of informal committed relationship with Thomas Blount. This is purely speculation, however, given how close Dudley and the queen were during the early years of her reign, they would've had ample opportunity to meet and perhaps even fall in love. Affairs were commonplace at court, though any proof of transgression (i.e. being caught or becoming pregnant) was punished by the queen. The threat of banishment or imprisonment would've been plenty of inducement to keep a relationship hidden.

As Queen Elizabeth I never married, it was King

James VI of Scotland who inherited the English throne after her passing. He was the son of Mary, Queen of Scots. Mary, after countless attempts to overthrow Elizabeth, was executed after spending nineteen years in captivity.

This is a work of fiction meant to entertain. Throughout my novel, I worked to blend fact and fiction together. For example, Queen Elizabeth did use a knife to slash the first letters patent drawn up for Robert Dudley. She was also the one honoured with the task of dealing the killing strike when out hunting. However, the details surrounding that event have been altered to accommodate my story.

Lady Katherine Grey married the Earl of Hertford in secret and, as a result, was imprisoned for the rest of her life. Her sister, not mentioned here, suffered a similar fate. Until their deaths, many wondered if they would be next in line for the throne.

Dorothy's family would eventually fall into obscurity. By the mid-sixteen hundreds, they would even lose the title of Baron of Stafford. Nonetheless, I see her story as one of success and determination in the face of adversity.

I hope you have enjoyed stepping into the world of the Tudors.

Printed in Great Britain
by Amazon